COLD STEEL

Professional fighting man Carter O'Brien can stick around Scot's Post, California, and risk taking a bullet . . . or he can ride up into the treacherous winter-locked mountains on an impossible mission of mercy. Because he has never been one to pass up a challenge, he chooses the mountains. The dangers are plenty — ambushers, marauding Indians, the worst kind of weather imaginable, and a deadly killer. In order to survive all that, O'Brien learns pretty quick that the job he's signed on for will require all the cold steel he has in him . . .

BEN BRIDGES

COLD STEEL

Complete and Unabridged

LINFORD
Leicester

First published in Great Britain in 1995

First Linford Edition
published 2018

A catalogue record for this book is available
from the British Library.

ISBN 978–1–4448–3724–7

Published by
F. A. Thorpe (Publishing)
Anstey, Leicestershire

Set by Words & Graphics Ltd.
Anstey, Leicestershire
Printed and bound in Great Britain by
T. J. International Ltd., Padstow, Cornwall

This book is printed on acid-free paper

1

Carter O'Brien stared down at the threadbare carpet and tried not to yelp while the doctor stitched him up.

He was a stranger to Scot's Post, California. He'd only been in town a few hours. But the doctor had him figured pretty good when he said, 'I guess this is all in a day's work to you, eh, Mr. O'Brien?'

O'Brien made no reply, afraid to speak in case he yelled instead. But he thought he knew what the doctor meant. You only had to look at his wind-bronzed face, fist-battered from a short spell as a prizefighter twenty years before and a thousand dangerous jobs ever since, to see that he and trouble were on first-name terms.

But the doctor had seen his scarred chest too, when he stripped off his bloody shirt to reveal the latest in a long line of wounds. And of course, he'd noticed the hang of O'Brien's businesslike .38 Colt Lightning the minute he'd walked into the surgery.

He sighed eloquently as the doctor continued to ply his needle and thread. The only other sounds were the ticking of the clock on the mantel and the mournful howl of the wind outside.

He'd been a fool to refuse the whiff of nitrous oxide he'd been offered earlier. But he'd heard stories about that stuff; about how, in the name of entertainment, they made buffoons out of people under its influence back east. And anyway, he preferred to keep his wits about him whenever possible.

At last the medic tied off the catgut in his upper left arm with one final, eye-watering tug, then trimmed off the excess with a dainty pair of scissors, and the pain subsided to a dull throb. A moment later the doctor blotted sweat away from the still-inflamed wound in his left biceps, examined it critically in the smoky, guttering lamplight, then nodded with satisfaction.

'Mr. O'Brien,' he declared with mock sobriety, 'I have some good news for you. I think you are going to live.'

O'Brien cracked a sour smile at him, relieved that the stitching was over. 'Thanks.'

'A dollar seventy-five is all the thanks I require,' the doctor replied, turning away with a kidney dish filled with bloodied swabs of cotton wool in his hand.

O'Brien got up off the worn-leather examination table and dug into the pocket of his corduroy pants. He was slim and long-legged, still compactly muscular despite the fact that he was rapidly approaching forty. After a moment he threw a quarter-eagle onto the doctor's cluttered desk and told him to keep the change.

Slowly he eased into the spare flannel shirt he'd fetched from his saddlebag and winced as he felt the stitches pull.

He buttoned up his old sheepskin jacket next, then clapped his tobacco-brown Stetson onto his close-cropped salt and pepper hair and headed for the door.

'Try to rest it for a while,' the doctor advised, gesturing to the wound. 'Come back in a week or so and I'll take those sutures out for you. No extra charge.'

O'Brien nodded. 'Sure, doc. If I'm still around.'

The doctor eyed him sidelong, then nodded in sudden understanding. 'I was forgetting,' he said. 'Well, I can't say as I blame you. I heard about what happened, of course. Whole town's talking about it. Just between you and me, I think *I'd* prefer to move on as well, if staying meant a confrontation with John Bragg.'

O'Brien's face hardened a bit at mention of the name, and he reached up to scratch at one cauliflower ear. 'Bragg's got nothing to do with it,' he replied quietly.

He let himself out of the surgery and

closed the door behind him.

In the alleyway outside, he saw that early November darkness had already stolen across the town, even though it wasn't much past six o'clock yet. He smelled snow on the strong northerly wind, too. The weather was turning at last. After a mild autumn, it looked as if winter was coming with a vengeance.

Tugging up the collar of his jacket with his right hand, he considered his next move. Before he did anything else, he had to find lodgings somewhere. He hadn't planned to overnight in Scot's Post, but circumstances had conspired to delay him. Besides which, he'd lost a fair amount of blood in that earlier scuffle, even though the wound itself wasn't serious, and now its effects were starting to catch up with him. A warming whiskey or two, some good hot food and a peaceful night's sleep, and he'd likely feel more like moving on tomorrow.

Scot's Post was a middling-sized agricultural community nestled up to the foothills of the Sierra Nevada, a combination of squat adobe structures very much in the Mexican style, and taller, more weathered board buildings. As soon as he reached Main, however, his robin's-egg blue eyes were drawn away to the east, where the chopped granite planes of the mountains shelved skyward twenty miles distant.

The Sierra Nevada, just part of a chain of mountains that extended for more than a thousand miles, dominated the view. Snow had already fallen across much of the rocky, timbered slopes that he could see, but it was difficult to tell if it was just a light covering or, more likely, drifts of ten or fifteen feet. From the look of the low-hanging heavy gray clouds bunching overhead, however, one thing was sure; there was still plenty more to come.

In a way, he thought, that was good. Because if the weather turned bad enough, this John Bragg he'd heard so much about might decide to stay at home. He certainly hoped so. He wasn't afraid of the man, but he didn't want any more trouble. One killing today had already been enough.

Another surge of wind buffeted him just then, and he shivered. That was the trouble with living this far north. The wind was constantly blowing down through the low passes and on across the chilly Feather River to swat at you with its icy fist.

He shivered again and turned onto Main, his breath smoking around his cold-reddened face, the eyes beneath the line of his hat constantly on the move, just in case Bragg was already here. Errant snowflakes spiraled to earth around him, and mercury was probably tumbling in every thermometer in the high country. For that reason he decided to stop a while in the first saloon he came to, a place called The Paradise, where about fifty other men were already seeking refuge from the inclement weather.

Just inside the doorway he paused a moment while his eyes adjusted to the

light and he surveyed his new surroundings. Lard-oil lamps hanging at
regular intervals from the low tin ceiling
illuminated a long, confined room with
dusty wood paneling and a bar that ran
along the back wall. The sawdusted area
between the bar and the door was
cluttered with round, baize-topped
tables and old ladderback chairs, while
a black stove squatting in the centre of
the room belched welcome heat to
every corner.

Unbuttoning his jacket, he crossed to
the bar and ordered a glass of Forty
Rod. The bartender's eyes flickered to
his blood-smeared sleeve before he
turned to reach a bottle down off the
shelf behind him. Obviously the doctor
had been right. The whole town
must've heard about what had happened earlier. But wisely the bartender
had refrained from comment, which
suited O'Brien fine.

As he put some coins down on the
counter and waited for his drink to
arrive, he noticed that the saloon also

8

dispensed coffee in the cold weather, and ordered a cup of that, as well. Around him, the comfortable chatter which had filled the saloon when he'd first walked in seemed to have dropped a notch, and all at once the place didn't seem to be as crowded as it had before.

He let the heat melt some of the snow on his broad shoulders and unfreeze the blood in his face so that his skin started to tingle. The twin order of whiskey and coffee came and O'Brien took an appreciative sip of the Forty Rod, then tipped the rest into his coffee. He took the cup over to a small, vacant table along the left-side wall and sank gratefully into a creaking chair, being careful to keep his back to the wall and the rest of the room in view.

He felt tired. That was the blood loss. But the whiskey-laced coffee tasted good; even the throbbing in his arm seemed to respond to it. And when he rolled and lit a cigarette, he began to feel even better. But even now he couldn't allow himself to relax completely. And not just because of John Bragg. It just wasn't in his nature to lower his guard so easily.

O'Brien was a cautious man, sometimes overly so. But then, in his line of work, he could hardly afford to be otherwise. For life-on-the-line danger was O'Brien's trade. He was a professional adventurer who took on every kind of risky job you could imagine — and a few you couldn't . . . but only when the job and the payment were right.

Not that he was just another hired gun. No; he was too complex a man to be so easily categorized. In truth, he was a paradox, even to himself. For though he lived a rough and often violent existence, he was not a cruel or vengeful man. He well knew the difference between good and bad, right and wrong, and while he made a bad enemy, as a friend he was second to none. He simply earned his living, a good living, the best and most satisfying way he knew how.

But hell, he thought ruefully, how he had to work at it sometimes! Take today, for instance, the job he'd been on for the past week. A freighting outfit in Sutter Creek had hired him to chase up a few long-standing debts for them. It should have been simple. And it was . . . until he'd reached Scot's Post earlier this afternoon.

Up until then, he'd passed through one town after another, visited one storekeeper or merchant after another, shown them his letter of authority, received payment or part-payment and signed receipts in his usual flowing copperplate. No trouble, no arguments, just a nice, easy little job.

But somewhere along the line word must have gone out ahead of him; that he'd been collecting on bad debts and was thus carrying a hefty payroll. Although he didn't know it, he became a target that two of the local low-lives found impossible to resist.

They'd jumped him in a long, narrow

alleyway on the south side of town. It was a dull, overcast day, and the alley was in deep shadow. Furthermore, piled crates and other stacks of refuse had offered his would-be assailants a dozen and one places to hide.

Face it, O'Brien, he told himself now, as he watched a few more men leave the saloon, each casting a nervous glance in his direction as they went. *You were careless. Damn careless. And it could have been the death of you.*

The first he'd known about it was a sudden flicker of movement from the corner of one eye, as the first of them thrust himself out of the shadows with an inarticulate snarl.

Instinctively O'Brien had backed up, away from him, guessing his intention and figuring to deal with him head-on. But even as he did so, a second would-be robber materialized right beside him.

Before he could react to that, white-hot pain slashed across his upper left arm. He groaned. Too late he realized that the first man was carrying a knife.

The long, thin blade reflected weak daylight as it came down again.

But by then O'Brien had shoved the pain to the back of his mind and was lunging forward, grabbing for the wrist of the hand that held the weapon. Gripping it hard, he'd sent his right fist into the man's armpit, buried it good and firm, then gave a jerk and dislocated the arm at the shoulder.

The low-life had screamed high, like a woman, and O'Brien had doubled him over with a jab to the stomach to shut him up. The robber fell to his knees, cradling his useless arm, begging for mercy. But O'Brien paid him no further mind because he was no longer a threat. Instead he turned to face the second man . . . only the second man had undergone a sudden change of heart, and was legging it towards the other end of the alley.

O'Brien's Colt had come into his palm as if by trickery, the short, deadly blue barrel pointing skyward as he yelled, 'Hold it or I shoot!'

Hard on the heels of his shout came the expected gunshot — but from an unexpected source. The bullet slapped into the board wall just to one side of where O'Brien stood, and as he spun around in surprise, splinters rained down on his hat and shoulders.

Automatically he threw himself down into a roll, cursing as he told himself that the first of his assailants hadn't just come armed with a knife — the bastard had a gun on him as well.

Another gunshot blasted along the alley as he rolled across the cold, rutted earth. He saw flame spit from the weapon's dark, stubby barrel, heard the bullet thud into an empty crate, and twisted some more. Then, all at once, he was back on his belly, thrusting up onto one knee, extending the Lightning to arm's-length, yelling, 'Drop it!'

The other man's face only screwed up some more and he jabbed his gun at

14

O'Brien again, determined to have another try.

The hell with that!

O'Brien got there first. He fired once, and the Colt jumped in his hand. The other man, still down on his knees a dozen feet away, suddenly hunched up, went, 'Aaaaahhh,' grabbed his chest with the hand holding the gun and then toppled over backwards.

He didn't move again.

Climbing to his feet, O'Brien threw a look behind him. The second man was no longer anywhere in sight.

It was all over, then.

Swearing softly, hating what he had been forced to do, he picked up his fallen hat and went to have a closer look at the man whose life he had just taken. The man was tall, thin, whiskery, with shaggy dark hair and a long nose. O'Brien noticed vaguely that he had bad, gappy teeth; that his dark eyes had rolled up into his head and stayed there. Blood was spreading

15

slowly across the front of his newish box jacket.

He was about twenty.

Jesus, little more than a kid.

O'Brien shook his head and put his own gun away. Suddenly he felt exhausted and restless. It was the same every time he used the awesome power that Colonel Colt's invention had given him. He took no pleasure in the act of killing. It repelled him. He understood that in such wild and ungovernable times, men lived by the law of the jungle. It was kill or *be* killed. But that didn't mean he had to like it. Or that it made the knowledge that he had taken yet another life any easier to bear.

Eventually the long silence that followed the exchange of gunfire had brought the inevitable bunch of rubber-neckers out to plug up the alley-mouth. Ignoring them, O'Brien leaned against one wall and waited for the arrival of the Scot's Post marshal. His left arm started throbbing. Blood dropped down off the tips of his fingers. Even though his jacket had absorbed much of the cut, he had a nasty feeling that the wound was going to need stitching.

Hell, that was a lot to look forward to.

The marshal arrived in fairly short order and pushed through the crowd with a shotgun in his hands. Quickly he identified the body. Then came the usual run of questions and answers, before the marshal finally asked O'Brien to step over to his office. There, more answers followed more questions. At last, O'Brien was allowed to go find a doctor who could stitch up the wound in his arm.

All of which had served to delay him so that now he had no choice but to stay overnight instead of moving on to the next town on his list, as had been his intention — a decision that was hardly going to endear him to the marshal, Milt Frazier.

'Mister,' Frazier had said earlier, in the privacy of his office, 'was I you, I'd get that arm doctored, then saddle up and get the hell out of here, lickety-split.'

Frazier was a tall, flat-bellied thirty-five-year-old with a thin face and short, oiled black hair. O'Brien frowned at him from the visitor's chair on the other side of the lawman's big desk. At length he said, 'Marshal, I'm not getting the hell out of *anywhere* lickety-split, not with *this* arm.'

'Well you'd better.'

'Why?'

'Because that feller you killed back there . . . that was Arnie Bragg, mister.'

'Is that supposed to mean something?'

Frazier got up and took a restless turn around the square, sturdy office, then came back over and perched himself on the edge of the desk, right in front of O'Brien. Reaching a decision, he drew in a deep breath and said quietly, 'I'm gonna tell you somethin' in confidence, O'Brien, and if you ever repeat it in public, I'll call you a liar right to your face. Arnie

Bragg was a good-for-nothin', shiftless, work-shy trouble-maker. You name it, I've arrested him for it. Drinkin'. Fightin'. Thievin'. Fornicatin'. He was a boil on this town's ass. Was you to cut him open, I suspicion he'd be bad right the way through.

'But for all that, Arnie was the apple of his brother John's eye. And I can guess how things're gonna run once John gets the news. It won't matter to him that you killed Arnie in self-defense. All that matters is that he's dead.' Frazier's eyes turned bleak as he said, 'John Bragg's gonna want a reckonin' with you, O'Brien.'

Awkwardly O'Brien finished rolling a cigarette. 'That's too bad, marshal. For *him*. Who is he, anyway? Big man around here?'

'Not so much big as mean. Him, his pappy, couple of cousins, they built up a stake workin' for the railroad — ay, and raisin' a few mail coaches along the way, I suspicion. Then, couple years ago, they bought some land about twenty miles west of town, hired some Mex labor and started growin' oranges. Pretty good oranges, matter of fact. But don't get to thinkin' that they're just like any other sodbusters you might've met along the way. They ain't. They're mean, like I say. They work them Mexes pretty thin. And they do pretty much whatever they like here in Scot's Post. It's easier that way. Less trouble.'

'And that includes attempted robbery and murder?'

That's the hell of this whole business, far as I'm concerned,' Frazier replied. 'If Arnie'd tried to rob you 'cause he needed the money, *that* I could understand. But the money didn't even come into it. I know exactly why he went for you in that alleyway — 'cause he was bored and out to raise a little Cain. Just 'cause it was somethin' to *do*.'

'Well,' O'Brien said, blowing smoke towards the ceiling, 'he sure won't have that problem ever again. But I'm serving you notice, marshal. If his brother tries to mix it up with me, young Arnie's just liable to have some unexpected company for the rest of eternity.'

'That's not funny, O'Brien.'

'It wasn't meant to be. I don't want any more trouble, you know that. But what happened to Arnie Bragg was his own stupid fault. I'm not going to be run out of town just because I killed him before he could kill *me*.'

Frazier made a helpless gesture with his hands. 'Look, I'm only tryin' to save everyone a heap o' grief here. I know how you feel. 'Course I do. But you're not gonna make things any easier by stickin' around town any longer than you have to.'

O'Brien had heard enough. He was fed up with bleeding all over the marshal's puncheon floor and he wanted to get his arm seen to. Getting to his feet, he reached over and crushed the cigarette butt out in Frazier's oyster-shell ash-tray. 'AH right, marshal. You've done your duty. You've warned me about Bragg. Now why don't you take it one step further, and go warn Bragg about *me*? That way we can both avoid each other till I'm ready to leave.'

'You don't warn men like Bragg. About *anything*.'

'In that case, it looks like we're getting nowhere fast.' He headed for the door. 'Be seeing you, marshal.'

Frazier watched him go. 'On your way out of town, I hope.'

Shaking his head at the memory, O'Brien took another sip from his steaming mug. He had long since stopped feeling guilty about what had happened to Arnie Bragg. You had to get things like that into perspective, and quickly, otherwise you'd go mad.

It was too bad that his partner had gotten away, though . . .

'Checkers, pilgrim?'

The sudden invitation disturbed O'Brien from his ruminations, and he turned to face the man sitting at the

22

table next to him. The old codger was sixty-five if he was a day, probably older, with a bony, well-weathered face that was all cheekbones and hooked nose and deep-set, wet green eyes. With one hand he gestured to the board and counters on the table in front of him, and picked at the fuzzy, dishwater-gray beard obscuring the lower half of his face with the other. Because he was practically toothless, his whiskery mouth looked as if it had caved in on itself.

'You play, son?' he asked.

'I play, granpaw,' O'Brien replied. 'But not right now, thanks all the same.'

'Got your mind on other things, I 'spect,' the old-timer muttered.

O'Brien said, 'What was that?'

The old man shrugged. 'Nothin'.'

At that moment, O'Brien heard the saloon door open with a distinctive squeak of hinges, and turned his head quickly, but it was only another couple of townsmen leaving. He took a drag at his cigarette and thought, *Jesus, I must be getting jumpy in my old age.*

A few minutes later the door opened again, and O'Brien's pale blue eyes returned to it. A thin man who was all but lost in a damp greatcoat hurried inside, and just before the door closed behind him, O'Brien saw that it was now snowing quite heavily.

'Don't worry, son,' said the old-timer at the next table, focusing his attention on the position of the checkers in front of him. 'I'll let you know when he arrives.'

O'Brien finished his coffee and pushed the cup away from him. 'When *who* arrives?'

'John Bragg.'

O'Brien snorted. 'Let me tell you something, granpaw. I'm not a vindictive man. But so help me, I'm gonna cloud up and rain all over the next person who mentions that name around me.'

The old man shifted one of the white checkers, then began to study the game from the black perspective. 'Now, no

need to get all nettled, son. I understand how it is. 'S only to be expected,
you gettin' all snappish. That's how
most any sensible man'd feel was he
just about to face — '

O'Brien raised one warning palm.
'Don't you dare say that name again
granpaw, not lessen you want to lose
the few teeth you've got left.'

The old man made another move,
took three white checkers in a string of
leapfrogs, then let loose a wheezing
cackle. 'That's it — threaten a poor,
defenseless old man.'

'You don't look so defenseless to me,'
O'Brien replied. 'Fact, I reckon you
could still piss vinegar, if you put your
mind to it.'

The old man turned his wet green
eyes back to O'Brien. 'Naw, naw. My
vinegar pissin' days is long gone, son.'

Relenting a little, O'Brien indicated
the board. 'Come on then, granpaw
— set 'em up again. If you're so old and
worn-out that I can't threaten you, the
least I can do is beat you at checkers.'

But now the old-timer shook his head, and his eyes twitched just a fraction so that he could focus on something behind O'Brien. 'Checkers is gonna have to wait, son,' he said quietly.

A tingle washed down over O'Brien's face and another trickled down his spine as he heard that distinctive hinge-squeak yet again. He turned slowly in his chair just as a veritable mountain of a man stamped into the saloon with three slightly smaller men behind him, and all at once the place grew so still and silent that you could hear the biting wind push at the saloon and rock it ever so slightly.

Leaning towards O'Brien in the manner of a conspirator, the old-timer whispered, 'That's — '

O'Brien muttered, 'Don't tell me.'

John Bragg.

John Bragg and the men with him swaggered deeper into the room and let the door slam shut behind them. Their long, heavy coats and broad-brimmed hats were whitened with snow. It trickled down their faces, dripped off their spur-bedecked boots, puddled on the sawdusted floor beneath them. Although Bragg appeared to be unarmed, the three men with him were all holding repeaters across their chests.

For a long beat they just stood there, looking around the room, almost enjoying the fear their arrival had aroused. The wind picked up again and O'Brien heard the clapboard walls groan. Overhead, the lard-oil lamps swayed gently, so that the whole scene took on an unreal, dreamlike quality.

When Bragg and his companions moved again, some of the men who had turned to watch them enter actually flinched. But they only went as far as the stove, where Bragg tugged off his gloves and held his big, hard-edged palms out to the cherry glow that was just visible behind the grille.

Unhurriedly then, Bragg worked the buttons of his Albert overcoat loose and carried on looking around the silent room. Beneath the overcoat he wore a red check woolen shirt and a shaggy gray sweater stuffed into baggy duck pants. The wind rose and fell again. Someone's belly rumbled. Someone else cleared a suddenly-clogged throat. Bragg's big face moved imperceptibly in the smoky, lemon-colored lamplight, his eyes tightened, his nostrils flared.

Finally he spoke. ''M looking for a man named O'Brien,' he said.

The wind howled some more. Snow pattered against the oilpaper windows. The swaying lamps whispered, *eek . . . eek . . . eek . . .*

Bragg waited for a reaction. There was none. Again, sterner, he said, ''M looking for a man named O'Brien.'

O'Brien pulled down a deep breath and said, 'You just found one.'

Bragg turned towards him, evaluated him swiftly with shrewd dark eyes and almost casually brushed the folds of his coat further aside to reveal the big Walker Colt sitting in the cracked-leather holster around his chunky waist.

'You'd be the O'Brien who killed my kid brother?' he asked bluntly.

O'Brien nodded.

'Then you're the O'Brien I been looking for.'

The silence was an almost palpable thing. Then, all of a sudden, chair legs scraped ruts into the sawdust as the bystanders quit their tables and quickly scampered out of the line of fire.

2

O'Brien studied each of the four men in turn. Bragg came first, of course. He was a giant, six-six easily, and big with it, maybe as much as two hundred seventy pounds. When he moved he moved awkwardly, just how you would expect a fat man to move, but somehow O'Brien got the impression that he wasn't so much fat as muscular, that it was almost as if he had too many slabs of muscle to carry easily.

He looked at the face beneath the big damp hat, gauged the man's age at somewhere around his own. Bragg had close-set brown eyes, a big, belligerent out-thrust of nose, a set of lips that were fixed into a curious amalgam of sneer and snarl beneath a big, untidy moustache and a square, granite-tough jaw.

Two of the three men with him were

Anglos, the third a Mexican. The first of them was big and stocky, though not so big and stocky when you compared him with Bragg. He was blond, pale-faced, hollow-eyed, with a sharp nose and a slash for a mouth. He was somewhere between his middle and late twenties.

The man standing next to him was a couple of years older and a few pounds lighter, dressed soberly in black, with hazel eyes and a very blond beard that gave him an almost Nordic cast.

A last O'Brien's eyes settled on the Mexican. Tall, thirtyish, slim as a whip even in his heavy winter jacket, dark-skinned and more handsome than any man had a right to be. His black eyes glittered in the lamplight and he showed teeth like pearls in a cool, sadistic grin as he returned O'Brien's scrutiny.

At last O'Brien said, sounding calmer than he felt, 'I've been expecting you, Bragg. Sit down, let me buy you a drink. I'll tell you how it was between your brother and me.'

Bragg made a kind of strangulated chuckle deep inside his throat and shook his head in wonderment at O'Brien's gall. 'I *know* how it was between my brother and you. You killed him.'

'It was him or me,' O'Brien replied simply.

'He was barely nineteen, O'Brien. Just a kid.'

'He was old enough to try robbing me,' O'Brien told him levelly. 'Old enough to cut me with a knife and then try to shoot me.'

Bragg eyed him sidelong and jabbed a big forefinger at him. 'You keep on bad-mouthing my brother that way and we'll finish you right here and now.'

O'Brien raised an eyebrow at him. 'Isn't that the intention?'

Bragg shook his head. 'Nuh-uh. 'The intention' is that we take you outside and hang you, O'Brien. That's 'the intention'.'

A collective gasp travelled around the

room, and Bragg ran his hate-filled eyes across the men who had made it, almost challenging them to stop him. 'You hear that?' he asked, raising an already stentorian voice. 'We're hanging this piece of scum for the murder of my little brother. Any objections?'

No one said a word, and looking around the room, O'Brien thought cynically, *Thanks.*

Turning his head to one side so that he could address the man with the beard, Bragg said, 'Take his belt gun, Aaron.'

With a nod, Aaron took a step around Bragg and started forward. O'Brien watched him come, wondering where in hell Marshal Frazier was hiding himself while all this was going on, and knowing he had better do something fast if he didn't want his neck stretched a couple of extra feet.

He got up and stood well-balanced, waiting for Aaron to come nearer, and seeing him do that, Aaron suddenly froze, uncertain about what he should do next.

There's been enough killing today,' O'Brien said softly, his eyes pinning those of Bragg.

Bragg snorted, 'You know, I *thought* that's what you'd say.'

'I mean it. Look, Bragg — I didn't relish the killing of your brother, but when it happened, you know as well as I do that he only got what was coming to him. Let that be an end to it.'

Bragg said in a voice that trembled slightly, 'Just keep it up, O'Brien. Just you keep soiling my brother's memory.'

Sick to death of everything that had happened today, O'Brien snapped, 'The hell with your brother's memory. I just don't want any more trouble.'

Bragg said, 'Maybe it's just that you don't like the odds so much now.'

'The odds've got nothing to do with it.'

Bragg's sneer-snarl mouth worked itself into a cool grimace. 'I think they *have,*' he countered with quiet confidence, ''Cause no matter how sudden you might think you are with that gun of yours, even *you* can't buck four-to-one odds.'

'Want to bet?'

By way of answer, Bragg started walking slowly towards him, past Aaron, pushing and heeling chairs and tables out of his path without once taking his eyes off O'Brien. 'All right,' he invited. 'Try it.'

Watching him come closer, hearing the floorboards groaning under his weight, O'Brien began to wonder if Bragg wasn't crazy as well as mean. He had the damnedest feeling that he'd underestimated the man, and cursed his decision not to ride on while he still had the chance.

'You take another step,' he said in a low, deadly tone, 'and you'll be the first to drop.'

Bragg nodded equably enough. 'Daresay I will. Big enough target, after all.' Then his eyes went heavy-lidded as he added in a harsher tone, 'But the minute you shoot me, my boys here'll open fire too — at all these *other* fellers.'

Another gasp went through the men bunched together up at the bar as Bragg's companions brought their repeaters around on them. O'Brien saw their eyes widen, heard a couple of them mutter Bragg's name as they shook their heads and shuffled their feet and implored him not to shoot them.

Ignoring them, still advancing, Bragg said, 'You want all *their* blood on your hands as well, O'Brien?'

O'Brien wanted to say, *You're bluffing*. But somehow he didn't think Bragg was bluffing at all. Quickly his eyes darted back to the frightened men now crowding even closer together along the length of the bar. One of them muttered placatingly, 'C-come on now, Big John . . . you don't wanta hurt us . . . '

Bragg said, 'Well? How about it, O'Brien?'

On the surface, it wasn't really much of a threat. O'Brien owed these townsmen no more consideration than they had already shown him. But whether he did or not, whether Bragg was bluffing or not, he couldn't risk letting Bragg make good on his threat, not and still live with himself afterwards. He just wasn't built that way.

With a tactician's brain, O'Brien swiftly considered the fix he was in. Even weakened and slowed down as he was by the injury he'd sustained earlier, he figured he could still draw his Colt and kill Bragg and maybe one of the other men with him before the remaining two could react. That might be enough. With Bragg out of the picture, the survivors might be shocked into surrendering.

But that was a big *if*. And *if* on the other hand, they started shooting back, some of these bystanders were going to get hurt. Bad.

Another townsman said uncertainly, ' . . . B-BigJohn . . . ?'

There was only one alternative left — to take this argument outside, away from the townsmen. Outside, in the storm, with only himself to look out for, he might just be able to turn the tables.

Some of the rigidity went out of O'Brien's shoulders as, at last, he nodded in defeat. He put his hands up, hating to do it, wincing as he felt the stitches in his left arm pull again. 'All right, Bragg. You win.'

Bragg came to a halt on the other side of O'Brien's table. He dwarfed the man he had come to hang. O'Brien looked up at him, saw triumph light his dark eyes and thought, *That's it. Just you underestimate me the way I underestimated you.* And hard on the heels of that thought, *Where the hell are you, Frazier?*

Suspicion entered Bragg's gaze then. O'Brien had surrendered too easily, and he suspected a trap. His shaggy head tilted to one side as he tried to look deeper inside O'Brien's mind and see the truth. Steeling himself, O'Brien only returned his look, as the wind continued to buffet the otherwise silent saloon and the lard-oil lamps went, *eek . . . eek . . .*

Cautiously Bragg leaned forward and reached for O'Brien's Colt. He pulled the .38 from leather, examined it briefly, tucked it into his own belt, just behind the tarnished buckle.

'All right,' he growled. 'Head for the door, and no tricks.'

The old man sitting at the table next to O'Brien suddenly jumped to his feet. He was lanky and underweight, his sinewy arms and legs comically long beneath a worn-shiny buckskin shirt and fringed pantaloons. 'Now just you hold on a minute, Bragg — '

Bragg threw him a withering glance. 'This is none of your beeswax, Charlie Button,' he snarled. 'You stay out of it.'

And O'Brien added a warning of his own. 'Leave it, granpaw.'

But the old man, Charlie Button, shook his head. 'These other excuses for men might soil their britches ever' time you pass by, John Bragg, but me, I wasn't brought up in the woods to be scared by an owl. Your brother was a thievin' little bastard, and that's the plain truth of it. Not one man, woman or child in this town could find a good word to say for him, no — nor you, neither. But it's like this here feller said — Arnie got what was comin' to him, and me fer one, I'm glad of it.'

Bragg struck out with blinding speed, backhanding Charlie across the face with a fleshy crack and snapping his head sideways. The old man grunted and flopped back into his chair, blood spilling down over his shriveled bottom lip and on across his dirty gray beard.

O'Brien's fists clenched but he knew better than to submit to the rage inside him. This wasn't the time. But he looked at Bragg and told himself, *Outside, you big lug. Just wait till we're outside . . .*

As if reading his thoughts, Bragg turned his attention back to him and jerked a thick thumb towards the door.

'All right, O'Brien. Let's be moving.'

O'Brien edged out from behind the table and crossed the room on legs like wooden boards. He felt the eyes of the townsmen burning into his back as he strode towards the door. Another gust of wind pushed at the saloon and the structure swayed slightly under the force, the lamps swinging faster now, so that they threw shadows around the room like the ghosts of sailors on a storm-tossed fo'c'sle. He glanced over his shoulder once, saw Bragg and his cronies trailing him out. They were so sure of the power they wielded here that they weren't even bothering to keep an eye on the townsmen they'd just been threatening to kill. They knew there'd be no retaliation. The townsmen wouldn't dare.

He got to the door, opened it. Almost immediately the wind tried to snatch it away from him. An oblong of yellow light collapsed onto the porch and down into the street, illuminating the full ferocity of the blizzard. O'Brien slitted his eyes as he waded through the ankle-deep snow already gathering outside. Snow flurried and spiraled around him. The wind yanked at his hat, curling the brim even more. O'Brien saw four horses tethered to the hitch rack to his right, all of them standing with their rumps to the wind. He saw a length of rawhide rope coiled around the nearest pommel and knew a different kind of chill.

Quickly he scanned the street, hoping to find Frazier. But the rest of the street was deserted — and no wonder. The blizzard was reaching its full force now. Half the street-flares had gone out, leaving great patches of darkness right the way along Main, and what few flares remained alight were dancing crazily in the snowy gale, twitching yellow-orange light across the pristine whiteness that the thoroughfare had become.

Bragg and his companions followed him out onto the porch. The wind screamed on around them, nipping at their ears and making Bragg's unbuttoned overcoat flap like a bat in a sack. O'Brien kept his eyes on their shadows, which stretched out ahead of him.

He went as far as the edge of the porch and then hesitated, as if unsure what to do next. But in reality his muscles were coiled tighter than a landlord's heart and he was just biding his time, waiting for the right opportunity to —

Suddenly there was movement, little more than a blur, followed by a mixture of yells, one a screech of surprise, the other approximating an Indian war-cry. Taking advantage of the moment, O'Brien spun around just in time to see old Charlie Button flinging himself onto the Mexican, the two of them colliding, going forward, pitching headlong off the porch and into the piled snow, the Mexican's repeater going flying.

For three vital seconds, everything was confusion. The bearded man, Aaron, barked a question. His stockier counterpart's mouth dropped open. John Bragg started bellowing curses.

O'Brien, knowing he was never going to get a better chance, threw himself right at Bragg with a roar. The two of them met with a slap and went backwards until the saloon wall fetched them up short. 'The Paradise' swayed again, under the impact of Bragg's massive frame this time, and O'Brien actually bounced off him, but as he did —

His fingers closed around the Colt Bragg had stuffed into his belt and he yanked the gun free, leapt back, brought it up, triggered a shot into the porch overhang, where it dislodged gathering snow and sent it rumbling in a miniature avalanche down into the street.

His voice was a breathless yell. 'All right, back up, the lot of you! Throw down your weapons and get your hands up!' He chanced the briefest of glances over his shoulder, to where Charlie Button and the Mexican were still wrestling each other through the snow. 'That includes you too, mister!' he barked in Spanish.

Suddenly the storm-lashed area out front of the saloon seemed to stand apart from the rest of the town. Charlie Button kicked the Mexican away from him and sort of crawled through the snow to retrieve the fallen repeater. Slowly the Mexican got to his feet, fisting blood off his mouth and reaching for his discarded hat.

'You get on over here and join your friends,' O'Brien told him grimly, raising his voice to make himself heard above the wind.

As the Mexican climbed reluctantly back onto the porch, Bragg spat blood and took a pace forward that flattened the creaking snow underfoot. O'Brien's gun immediately twitched around to face him. 'I mean it, Bragg! Way I see it right now I don't need too much of an excuse to shoot you down!'

One of the others tossed his rifle

aside and put his hands up. 'You better do it, John.'

Bragg swore. 'The hell I will!'

O'Brien suddenly moved in fast, remembering the promise he'd made to himself just after Bragg had hit Charlie Button. His Colt became a gray, metallic blur. Bragg staggered under its clubbing force and floundered back-wards, clutching a ruined mouth and swearing wetly.

'Throw down your weapons!' O'Brien ordered. 'All of them!'

Aaron threw down his repeater, then he and the others loosened their jackets and reached gingerly for their handguns and some pretty wicked-looking knives, all of which quickly sank under their own weight into the snow.

'You all right, granpaw?' O'Brien asked.

Charlie was still down on one knee, breathing hard and using the Mexican's rifle as a prop. Without looking up he croaked, 'Yeah.'

'All right, break it up there!'

O'Brien identified the voice of the man who was only now struggling across the snowy street towards them, and shook his head. When the man pulled up in the high snow along the edge of the porch, he said, 'You took your own sweet time showing up, didn't you, Frazier?'

The marshal was holding his shotgun in thickly gloved hands across his chest. He squinted up at Bragg and the others, face held taut against the onslaught of the driving snow. 'What in the Sam Hill is goin' on here, Big John?' he demanded, as if he didn't know already.

Bragg said through his bloody mouth, 'Best you arrest this killer, Frazier. Not right, him walking around free when he killed my brother just this afternoon.'

Frazier said tiredly, 'This man killed Arnie in self-defense, John.'

'For crissakes!' Bragg exploded. 'Look what he just did to *me*, dammit! Arrest him, damn you, or else me and the boys here — '

'You and the boys there will climb onto your horses and get the hell out of town,' O'Brien cut in, speaking through clenched teeth. 'And I'd better not see any of your ugly faces again before I leave town tomorrow.'

Bragg turned his wide eyes onto Frazier, suddenly assuming the role of aggrieved citizen. 'You just gunna stand by and let him threaten us that way, Milt?' he demanded.

Lights were showing at windows and doorways all along Main now, and a few hardy souls were even venturing into the street to hear what all this was about. Sucking down a deep, cold breath, Frazier said, 'I think you'd better just go on home, John.'

'And what about our guns?' asked Aaron.

'I'll take those,' Frazier replied, clearly uncomfortable at having to take a stand against the Bragg faction. 'Fetch 'em back out to your place in a day or so.'

Bragg shook his head slowly in warning. 'Aw no,' he breathed. 'We're not going *anywhere* without our guns.'

'And we're sure not about to get too far in *this* weather,' added the Mexican, still glaring at Charlie.

Frazier said, 'Just go on home, Big John. I know you're upset about — '

'You're taking his side against us, Milt?' asked Bragg.

A moment of truth was reached then. Frazier's snow-caked hat bobbed in a nod. 'Yeah, I guess I am.'

Bragg glared at him for a long moment, as ice glittered on his eyelashes and blood crystallized on his big hard chin. Then Aaron put a gloved palm on his arm and urged him across the porch toward their horses.

'I won't forget this, Frazier!' Bragg spat over one shoulder.

The Scot's Post marshal watched him go, a worried look on his thin face. 'No,' he muttered. 'I don't guess you will.'

Bragg and his companions brushed

snow off their saddles and swung aboard. As one, they turned their horses west and walked them slowly past and on out of town, huddled in their thick coats, heads down, thoughts doubtless dark and full of spite.

With the trouble over, at least temporarily, townsfolk began to disappear back indoors. At last Frazier released his trapped breath in a hiss and said, 'Goddamn, O'Brien! Didn't I tell you somethin' like this — '

'Save it, Frazier. I'm not in the mood for a lecture.'

O'Brien slipped his Colt away and brushed past him to go down into the street and help Charlie Button to his feet. The old man seemed hardly to weigh a thing as he slowly got his long, thin legs under him. When he was able to support himself, O'Brien reached out and brushed snow off his sloping shoulders. 'Obliged to you, granpaw,' he said.

Charlie glanced up at him, pale face stippled by melting snowflakes. He wore a look that was hard to define. 'Didn't do it for you, son,' he replied shortly, then shuffled back up onto the porch and back into The Paradise.

O'Brien watched him go, thinking that maybe it was just reaction setting in, that the old man was only now realizing what a damn-fool dangerous thing he'd done for a total stranger.

He shivered and drew his unbuttoned jacket together, then made to help Frazier collect up Bragg's arsenal and carry it back to the lawman's office. Even before his fingers touched the first of the repeaters, however, Charlie Button turned in the saloon doorway and stuck out one long arm to point away to the east with a bony finger and call, 'Hey, marshal. Is my eyes playin' tricks on me, or do *you* see what *I* see?'

Both the marshal and O'Brien turned in the direction Charlie was indicating. Squinting hard into the uncertain darkness, O'Brien saw nothing and almost swung back to say as much. But then —

— a movement.

He looked again, closer. No, he was mistaken. It was just the flickering light, the twisting, tumbling mass of snow —

There!

O'Brien saw him clearer this time, a man, hatless, staggering down the centre of the street no more than a hundred-twenty yards away! The wind was battering him one way, then the other, but still he kept plowing through the thick snow, leaving two ragged gray lines behind him, head hanging loosely on one sloping shoulder, arms hanging limp at his sides, obviously exhausted and yet somehow finding the strength to keep on putting one wet-through boot in front of the other . . .

O'Brien murmured, 'That's a *man* out there.' Then, louder, 'That's a *man* out there!'

He jumped down off the porch and into the full force of the storm, running as fast as he could up the street to reach the man who now looked as if he'd just about run out of string. Frazier followed him out at a slippery lope, and together they closed on the apparition just as he finally gave up and collapsed face-first into the snow.

O'Brien reached him first, went down on his knees and hauled the man over onto his lap, but it was impossible to make out any important details. The man's head lolled lifelessly. His clothes were saturated, his face bristly, gaunt, wind-burnt and sore-looking. His eyes rolled wildly, his mouth opened and closed without a sound —

Frazier came panting up just then, kicking up snow all around him. He bent and peered at the man, examining him as best he could in the poor light and atrocious weather. O'Brien said, 'Know him?'

The fellow was about twenty. His black hair hung in strands across his ice-encrusted forehead. Frazier shook his head and said, 'He's not from around here.'

'Then where the hell'd he come from?'

The marshal looked briefly at the young man's boots. They were worn down, scuffed raw, almost falling apart. Then his eyes travelled up to the far, jagged mountains, hidden now behind the wall of snow. 'If I didn't know better . . . '

'What?'

His voice trailed off and he reached down to lend a hand. 'Come on, let's get him over to my place.'

Between them they got the near-unconscious newcomer up and hoisted him across the street and into Frazier's office, which was nearer than the doctor's surgery. They stretched him out on one of the bunks in Frazier's cell-block and covered him with a blanket. He was trembling like a man in the grip of a fit, and his teeth were chattering like castanets.

Frazier went outside to fetch him a mug of good hot coffee. O'Brien headed back to the door, intending to get the doctor.

As he put his hand on the doorknob,

Frazier stopped him with a warning. 'Watch yourself out there, O'Brien. The day John Bragg lets me post him out of town without a fight hasn't dawned yet.'

'You saying you think he's still out there?'

'I *know* he's still out there. And armed again, I shouldn't wonder.'

O'Brien nodded soberly. 'I'll steer clear of darkened alleys,' he replied. Then he went to fetch the doctor.

There wasn't a whole lot he could do after that except clutter up Frazier's office, so he left Frazier and the doctor to it and went back out into the squall to locate a restaurant and get some supper and then find himself a room for the night.

The blizzard continued to batter the town right through what remained of the evening and on into the long, snowy darkness. Every time it seemed as if it might die down, it suddenly picked up again and, if anything, grew worse. But around two or three in the morning it finally blew itself out, and then an eerie peace slowly settled back over Scot's Post.

O'Brien rose early next morning. His left arm was stiff and sore, but he'd expected that. He washed, dressed and took a cautious glance out at the town through his condensation-smeared window.

Scot's Post lay still and silent beneath a pure white mantle. Icicles hung from porch overhangs like shards of glass. Trough-water had frozen into blocks of solid ice. Thin white clouds streaked from north to south across the otherwise blue sky, but O'Brien didn't care much for the looks of the heavier gray masses that had draped themselves across the peaks to the east, and appeared to be congregating in preparation for yet another onslaught.

He went downstairs and out onto the quiet nearly-deserted street. Snow drifts were everywhere, ranging in depth from two feet to ten or twelve. He paused on the boardwalk, tested the air with sensitive nostrils and concluded that as much as he wanted to push on, he'd be a fool to try it today.

He returned to the restaurant he'd patronized the night before and ordered breakfast. Afterwards he trudged uptown to the livery stable at which he'd quartered his half-wild little mustang the previous afternoon and paid for its care for another few days.

On the way back down he stopped off at Scot's Post's only bank and deposited all the debt money he'd collected so far. He'd learnt the hard way what kind of a temptation that could be; for the duration of his stay in town — and the weather was going to dictate however long that would be — it was safer in a vault.

With all his chores done by the middle of the morning, he headed for The Paradise, hoping to find Charlie Button. The saloon was catering mostly to the coffee-drinking trade when he got there, men the weather had rendered idle for one reason or another. When he spotted the old man sitting at his usual table, poring over another one-sided game of checkers, he crossed to the bar, paid for two mugs of coffee and took them over to him.

'Morning, granpaw,' he greeted, sitting down opposite the other man. Gesturing to the board he said, 'Set 'em up and I'll give you that game I promised you.'

Charlie turned his wet green eyes onto him without noticeable enthusiasm. He was dressed much as he'd been the night before, save for the addition of a bulky red and gray blanket jacket that looked to be of Indian manufacture. A scab showed blackly on his lip, where Bragg had hit him.

'Fancy your chances, do you?' he asked as his thin vein-threaded hands shifted the checkers back to a starting position.

O'Brien's mouth moved in a gentle smile. 'Well, let's just say I'm quietly confident.'

Charlie moved first. 'Thought you was pullin' out today,' he remarked idly.

O'Brien slid a checker from one square to another. 'So did I, till I took a look out my window this morning.' He looked up at the old-timer. 'I'm obliged to you, Charlie,' he said. 'For what you did last night.'

Charlie shrugged and made another move. 'Ferget it. I have.'

'Well, just so you know.'

'An' jus' so's you know,' the old man echoed, dropping his voice and leaning forward across the board. 'They're still here, in town. Bragg an' the others.'

O'Brien had half-suspected as much, but having it confirmed still made his short hairs stir. 'You seen 'em around?'

Charlie nodded. 'While you an' the marshal was bringin' that pilgrim in outten the storm las' night, they come ridin' back up the street, took up their weapons, then lit out.'

'Where to?'

He gave another shrug. 'Oh, they got friends in town who'd put 'em up for the night. Folks who'd be too skeered to do otherwise, I should say.' He waited for O'Brien to make another move, then countered it and said, 'I'd walk soft an' carry a real big stick if I was you, son. Bragg an' his kin — '

'I've already heard it, granpaw. Marshal Frazier let me have it chapter and verse.'

He took three of the old man's counters in as many leaps, and Charlie's skeletal, weathered forehead corrugated into a frown. 'Well, you watch out for 'em, anyway. They're not above back-shootin' a man, any of 'em. Bragg's the worst, though you likely figured that much out for yourself already. But them cousins of his, Tom and Aaron Quinn, they can be pretty mean too.

'After the Central Pacific started pushin' west, they found work as what you might call 'overseers', or foremen, on the railroad. I hear tell they kept them Chinese track-layers workin' from dawn till dusk, seven days a week, an' darn' — near stripped the hides off 'em if they complained about it afterwards. Fer sure I know they had more o' them Celestials die on the gangs they supervised than anyone else.

'Then there's Rafael da Silva, the Messican. Word has it that he useta be a gun-fer-hire down Sonora way. And they sure don't come no colder, nor more vicious. Got mixed up in politics a few years back, carried out a couple assassinations an' made Sonora too hot fer him, so he legged it up here. They say he's pretty sudden, an' I b'lieve 'em.'

After much deliberation, he finally shifted another counter and took one of O'Brien's checkers. O'Brien immediately responded with another string of leapfrogs that took three more of Charlie's counters.

The old man made a sound of disgust in his throat. 'Cheez, you sure play to win, don't you? I thought you said you was beholden to me?'

'I am.'

'Well, why'n't you *show* it ever' once in a — '

Suddenly the old man's face screwed up and he made a wheezing groan and hugged himself. O'Brien leaned forward, concerned. 'You all right, Charlie? What is it?'

Charlie gave another groan, clamping his mouth tight shut to stifle the sound. His eyes screwed down so taut that O'Brien actually saw the eyeballs themselves rolling beneath the thin, yellowish lids.

A moment more went past, and then the old man seemed to get himself back under control, and relaxed visibly. His eyelids snapped back and his wet green eyes fixed on O'Brien once more as he gave a tired nod. 'Ayuh, I'm . . . fine. Jus' . . . gettin' old . . . that's all . . . ' He reached up and sleeved a sheen of sweat off his face. 'I figger I sure could use somethin' stronger'n this coffee, though.'

O'Brien nodded and got to his feet. In less than a minute he was back with two shot-glasses filled with whiskey. 'Here, get this down you.'

The old man took his drink and made it vanish in two quick gulps. The liquor seemed to give him back some strength, and he began to set the counters up for another game without making any further reference to his recent infirmity.

Just then the door opened with its distinctive squeak and Marshal Frazier came in with a big, overweight man in a fur coat and a plug hat. O'Brien recognized the man as Peter McGovern, a storekeeper from whom he had collected an outstanding debt just yesterday afternoon.

Frazier and the storekeeper came to stand over them. Taking off his hat and running a splayed hand up through his short dark hair, the marshal said, 'Like a word, O'Brien, if you can spare us a couple moments.'

'Sure.'

Glancing at Charlie, Frazier said, 'It's kind of personal.'

Charlie waved one hand and said drily, 'Don't mind me, marshal. I'm hard o' hearin' anyway.'

Frazier and the storekeeper exchanged a look, then pulled up seats to join O'Brien and the old man at the table. Frazier came straight to the point. 'Mr. McGovern here's got a job he'd like to put your way.'

O'Brien turned his pale blue eyes onto the storekeeper and said, 'I've already got a job, Mr. McGovern.'

Frazier said, 'What, collectin' on bad debts? I'm talkin' about a *real* job, O'Brien; a risky one, sure, but one that pays pretty good.'

Frowning now, O'Brien said curiously, 'What kind of job?'

McGovern swallowed audibly and whispered, 'There's only one way to put it, Mr. O'Brien. It's a matter of life and death. To be precise, a matter of fourteen lives and deaths.'

3

Peter McGovern was a big fifty-year-old with a bald head, a thick handlebar moustache and very thick black eye-brows. As he unbuttoned his coat, there was no mistaking the concern that tightened the line of his faintly womanish mouth and made his sausage fingers clumsy. Leaning forward, he said quietly, 'That young man you and the marshal found wandering up Main Street last night, the one you took across to the marshal's office?' He said it as if it might have slipped O'Brien's mind. 'That was my nephew, Mr. O'Brien, my sister's eldest boy, David Conway.'

'How's he doing, McGovern? He looked pretty rough last night.'

McGovern pulled a kerchief from his pocket and mopped his florid face. He had a big nose and restless brown eyes.

A faint white scar sat on one of his massive eyebrows, the only blemish on an otherwise clear skin. 'He'll live. Barely. But Doc Wilmer thinks he might lose a couple of fingers to frostbite, and he's been driven half snow blind.'

'What was he doin' out in the middle o' that blizzard anyway, Peter?' asked Charlie, apparently forgetting his supposed deafness. 'I allus thought your folks lived in Nevada.'

McGovern glanced at him. 'They do . . . did.' He turned back to O'Brien. 'That's to say, my sister and her family lived in Piper Peak, which is about two hundred and fifty miles south and east, up until six weeks ago. You see, things haven't gone so well for my sister or her family of late, so I suggested that they come and start a new life for themselves out here. My brother-in-law, he was an Express company superintendent, but he lost his job and, well, what with one thing and another — '

Frazier took over. 'Cut a long story short,' he said, getting right to the heart of the matter, 'they left Piper Peak a month and a half ago, Mr. McGovern's sister, her husband and four children, and also her sister-in-law and *her* family. Only trouble is, they left it a little late in the season — '

'Well, it was a big decision to make,' the storekeeper cut in defensively. 'They just took longer than they should have to make it.'

Frazier waved that aside. 'Added to which,' he went on, 'it seems they badly underestimated the time they needed for each stage of the journey.' He put his elbows on the table and steepled his fingers. 'The upshot is, they got as far as Klamath Pass — that's about a hundred miles northeast of here, just the other side of the mountains — and then the snow came. Cut 'em off.'

McGovern bobbed his head anxiously. 'David managed to come on ahead to fetch help, and the way he tells it, the rest of them are in a pretty sorry state. They can't go forward and they can't go back. His aunt and one of her children are poorly, their guide has also gone snow blind and, of course, they're running out of supplies. If this weather turns any worse, I — I fear we may lose them all.' His voice cracked on the last word, and he dashed sudden tears from his eyes.

Contemplating the whiskey in his glass, O'Brien said, 'So you're looking for someone to take supplies back across the mountains to your folks and then get them out of there.' His eyes came up onto McGovern's face. '*Me.*'

'The marshal says you're just the man for the job,' McGovern confirmed. 'And of course, I'd be willing to pay you handsomely for your trouble.'

'There's just one problem, McGovern,' O'Brien replied. 'I'm not a miracle-worker. I can't do the impossible.'

'Eh?'

'From what I've seen of this weather and those mountains, a man would need a powerful lot of luck to go up there and expect to come down again in one piece. I saw the state of your nephew, don't forget. Just making the trip one way all but killed him. To go up there and hope to come back with — how many people all told, Frazier?'

Frazier said, reluctantly, 'Six adults, if you include the guide, and nine children.'

O'Brien sat back, his point made. 'I'd like to help you, McGovern, but it can't be done. Not by just one man. And certainly not by a man who's still favoring a bum arm.'

McGovern looked as if he'd just been slapped. He opened and closed his mouth a few times. Clearly he had not been prepared for O'Brien's refusal. He said desperately, 'It's *got* to be done.'

O'Brien gave it some more thought. 'Maybe a man *could* get supplies through to them. *Maybe*. But he'd never get that many greenhorns back across the mountains alive, not in these conditions and more snow on the way, even supposing the sick could be moved. No; he'd have to hole up with them until the weather breaks, which is something I'm not prepared to do.' He shook his head regretfully. 'I'm sorry, McGovern. I'd like to help, but I'll be candid with you — I'm not prepared to take the risk or the responsibility.'

The door opened again just then, and O'Brien glanced over one shoulder as John Bragg, his cousins and Rafael da Silva swaggered in and looked around. Suddenly it went absolutely silent in The Paradise, as watching townsmen held their breath and waited for all hell to break loose. Bragg's eyes found those of O'Brien and they traded stares for a long few seconds, Bragg reaching up to rub gloved fingers over the scabby bruise around his mouth.

A couple of townsmen grabbed their hats and left, skirting around the newcomers in order to reach the door. Watching them go, Bragg's moustache stirred as his lips pulled back to form a chilly, faintly menacing smile. Then his right hand moved suddenly and Frazier, sitting in a chair to O'Brien's right, stiffened as Bragg threw him a slow, sarcastic salute, then clattered across to the bar, boot heels sounding loud in the ominous silence.

After he ordered coffee, a low buzz of conversation started back up, though much quieter than before. Leaning close, Frazier hissed, 'I tell you, O'Brien, it would do you a lot of good to be someplace where John Bragg *isn't*, right now.'

O'Brien only replied mildly, 'And I suppose the idea of you going over there and reminding him that you posted him out of town last night is out of the question, huh?'

Irritably, Frazier said, 'Come on now, O'Brien. You know what I'm tryin' to say. We're talkin' about the lives of women and children here — '

'We're talking about a job that only a fool would undertake,' O'Brien replied. 'And even a fool would know he couldn't do it alone.' Softening his tone a little, he added, 'Look, maybe a few men, half a dozen maybe. Men who know the mountains, know how to look after themselves — '

'I'll do it.'

All eyes turned to Charlie Button, who was sitting back himself now, rolling his empty glass between his palms. McGovern snorted and shook his head. More diplomatically, Frazier said, 'Aw now, look here, Charlie. We appreciate the offer, but — '

Charlie snapped testily, 'But what?'

'You're too old, man.'

Now it was Charlie who snorted. 'Too old! Hell, you know me, marshal! I been trappin' an' tradin' for beaver since I was knee high to a splinter. Attended my fust rendezvous when I wasn't much more'n fourteen. Bridger, Beckwourth, the Soublette boys, I knowed 'em all at one time or another.'

McGovern said incredulously, 'Are you saying you used to be a mountain man, Charlie?'

'Tarnation, I've spent most of my *life*

in mountains like them there bumps out yonder, *and* in weather that'd make this look more like summer in Death Valley. Why, I remember goin' over the Sierra Nevada with old Joe Walker back in '33 — '

With some urgency, Frazier interrupted him. 'Are you serious, Charlie? Do you *really* think you could pull it off?'

Charlie flicked a glance at O'Brien. 'Well, if he won't give 'em a whirl, I'll try it. An' whether you like it or not, McGovern, I'm just about the best you're gonna get. Who else'll risk it?' He made a disdainful sweeping gesture with one arm. 'Any o' these other brave souls?'

The marshal and the storekeeper exchanged another look. Then Frazier said, 'We'll, uh, consider your offer, Charlie. Let you know.'

'Well, don't leave it too long, fellers, not iffen them folks is as sick an' short o' food as you say they is. How long'd it take this here nephew o' yours to get down here, Peter?'

McGovern said, 'Little under a week.'

'And that was afoot?'

'He . . . he lost his horse after about . . . twenty miles. It fell, busted its leg.'

'Well, even on horseback, an' leadin' a couple pack-mules, it's gonna take me that long again to reach Klamath Pass. Then, a' course, I gotta *find* 'em. That is a powerful long pass, you know.' He shook his head sorrowfully. 'You gents best face it. You cain't afford to be picky. You ain't got the time.'

O'Brien's eyes shuttled between the lawman and the storekeeper. Their indecision was almost painful to witness. After a long moment McGovern finally caved in. 'Do you *really* think you can do it, Charlie?' he whispered.

Charlie said soberly, and with unshakeable sincerity, 'I'll do it or die tryin', Peter.'

But Frazier wasn't so sure. 'Now wait

a minute, Mr. McGovern,' he began.

McGovern raised a hand that quietened him. 'No, Milt. Charlie's right. Do you think they're going to *volunteer* for this task, any of these men? Can you think of anyone else who'd risk it?' Frazier's continued silence told them all that he could not. McGovern went on, 'All right, Charlie. It's all down to you.'

O'Brien drained his glass and pushed it away from him, knowing it was irrational for the old man's unselfish offer to shame him but feeling ashamed all the same. 'Aw hell,' he said in defeat, speaking quickly before he could change his mind. 'You might as well count me in too.'

As all eyes turned back to him he said irascibly, 'I told you before that one man couldn't do it alone. He'll need help.'

McGovern reached out and grabbed his wrist and squeezed it. 'God bless you, Mr. O'Brien,' he said, pathetic in his gratitude.

Unmoved by it all, Charlie Button said, 'All right, Peter — let's get down to the practicalities. I want two pack-mules fully loaded inside the hour, an' supplies enough fer me an' my new partner here. Think you can manage that?'

The storekeeper nodded. 'I'll get to work on it right away.'

'You do that,' Charlie replied with a scratch at his fuzzy beard. 'We'll meet you outside your place at noon.' He pushed arthritically to his feet and jabbed a finger at O'Brien. 'An' don't you keep me waitin', son.'

O'Brien shook his head sourly, unable to shake the notion that he had somehow been railroaded into this dangerous, crazy business. 'I won't,' he replied, 'granpaw.'

After they quit the saloon, O'Brien went up to his hotel room, got his gear together and then trekked back to the livery stable and saddled his horse for the coming journey. His old Texas double-rig, his ammunition-heavy war bag, his Winchester 'One-in-One-Thousand', they had all accompanied him on countless do-or-die missions in the past, but he had a nasty feeling that this latest might well prove to be the most dangerous.

Buckling up the saddle's two girths and then hauling on his calfskin gloves, he cursed the foolish pride that had made him go back on his original decision not to get involved. *You couldn't leave well enough alone, could you?* he told himself disparagingly. *You couldn't just let that crazy old graybeard go and commit suicide on his own. Oh no; you've got to go and commit suicide with him . . .*

Still, he was committed now. He had to see it through. And this wasn't the first time he'd cursed his altruistic streak, just like it wasn't the first time he'd ever tried to repay a man who'd taken his part in some quarrel or another. So he resigned himself to the inevitable and walked the mustang down to McGovern's store forty minutes later and found Charlie, Frazier and McGovern out front, waiting for him, alongside a whole passel of other townsfolk as well.

He drew up and nodded a greeting. Gesturing to the two heavily laden mules standing patiently by the tie-rack, tails twitching at the first flakes of a new snowfall, he said, 'Everything ready?'

McGovern nodded. 'Everything, including a bottle of cherry brandy to help keep your spirits up. I packed it all myself, and Doc Wilmer threw in some medicaments for the sick.'

O'Brien turned to Charlie. 'Well, I guess we might as well get started, eh, granpaw?'

Charlie was sitting on a beat-up zebra dun, his long legs dangling straight down, Indian fashion, his buckskin pants stuffed into knee-high, fur-lined moccasins. His bony, weathered face looked pale in the cold, his nostrils red, his ancient round-crowned hat held in place by a thick green scarf that was knotted under his whiskery chin. A weapons belt gathered his blanket jacket in at the waist; a big-bladed Bowie knife in a decorated beaded sheath on his left hip counterbalanced the heavy Colt's Dragoon that dragged at the holster on his right.

Charlie said, 'They sure ain't no sense to lingerin'.'

Frazier and McGovern came down off the steps to reach up and shake hands with them. A gray-haired woman O'Brien took to be McGovern's wife muttered, 'God bless,' and another woman in the crowd raised a hand and said, 'Good luck.' There were quite a few echoes to that sentiment.

Charlie nodded brusquely and took up the lines of the pack-mules. 'So long,' he replied, and together he, O'Brien and the mules peeled away from the store and started down the street at a slippery walk, headed for the distant mountains.

Heavily muffled men, women and children lined both sides of Main, watching them go in curious silence. Word of their little expedition had evidently travelled fast, just like it did about everything else in Scot's Post. O'Brien surveyed the sky and grimaced. The heavy slate-gray clouds had pushed down from the serrated peaks to blanket the town as well, and the gusting wind was enough to make a man's eyes water.

They left the town behind them and pressed on to the east, cutting ragged tracks through drifts as tall as their horses' bellies. Ahead, the Sierra Nevada loomed like a slumbering giant, scored by great sweeping tracts of Black oak, Ponderosa pine and incense cedar, dotted with slabs of seamed snow-capped granite and dark green shrub.

At last O'Brien glanced across at his companion and said, 'All right, granpaw. What's the plan?'

Charlie answered without moving out of the sunken-headed hunch he had fallen into. 'We keep these here animals puttin' one foot in front of the other till we get where we're goin',' he said briefly.

'I mean, how do you figure to get those greenhorns back here in one piece?' O'Brien persisted.

'Same principle,' Charlie answered unhelpfully. 'Albeit in ree-verse. We keep them greenhorns puttin' one foot in front of the other till we get *them* back *here*.'

'Just like that, huh?'

'Jus' like that.'

The old man reached behind him and pulled a brown-glass whiskey bottle from one saddlebag. He unstoppered it, took a pull, shuddered, then replaced the stopper and shoved the bottle back where it came from.

O'Brien shook his head. 'You sure are a careful man with your whiskey, granpaw,' he remarked.

Charlie barely glanced at him. 'You got any more sich insultin' observations you wanna share with me afore we go any further?' he asked.

'I guess not.'

'Glad to hear it. I never was a one to mix talkin' an' ridin'.'

'We ride in silence then, do we?'

'Now, how'd you ever guess that?'

At last the foothills enveloped them completely, and soon they were lost in the awesome immensity of the mountain chain. Snow fell steadily and brought its own peculiar brand of silence with it. Scanning the broken land ahead, O'Brien spotted the tracks of grizzly bear, mountain sheep, mule deer and badger. The snow eased off and they rode higher, splashing through pebble-bottomed streams in order to follow a barely discernible trail into thicker timber and on past giant redwoods, the trunks of which were bigger around than the average house. Still the hills shunted ever skyward ahead of them, alternately mottled with Douglas fir, red fir and Jeffrey pine.

An hour passed in silence. Their progress was surprisingly good. Then O'Brien put his eyes onto the man riding beside him and said, 'Think I'll ride out ahead, get the lay of the land.'

Charlie shook his head and stifled a yawn, and O'Brien realized that he'd been dozing. 'Eh? Wassat?'

'I said I think I'll ride out, take a look around.'

'No need fer that. This low down, the travelling easy. It's when we git higher up that we'll have to ride wary. That's where the snow drifts the deepest, see. You lose one o' these mules in a drift fifteen, twenty feet deep, you'll waste a day jus' tryin' to find him again.'

O'Brien chewed his lower lip. 'I think I'll take a look up ahead, anyway.'

Charlie's snowy shoulders lifted and dropped in a shrug. 'Suit yerself.'

O'Brien left the old man behind him. When he came back twenty minutes later, spraying snow everywhere, Charlie was just slipping his bottle back into his saddlebag. The old man was swaying slightly, and his green eyes were glazed.

'You all right, granpaw?' O'Brien

asked sharply, a little irritated by the other man's intemperance.

Charlie focused on him and nodded. 'What'd you find up ahead?' he wheezed.

O'Brien used his chin to indicate their surroundings. 'More of the same.'

'What'd I tell you? Could've saved yerself some extry ridin' if only you'd listened to ol' Charlie.'

Turning his mustang, O'Brien fell in beside his crotchety companion. 'Best we spell the animals for a while,' he said, running a palm along his mount's neck. 'There's some timber up ahead that'll give us some decent shelter.' Pointedly he added, 'We can brew up some coffee.'

Charlie gave him no argument with that, so they continued to pick their way slowly up through all the clusters of sagebrush, chaparral and chamiso until what passed for a trail eventually sliced through a vast belt of fir trees that rose diagonally across a steep slope and gradually thinned to reveal the higher, sparser ridges above. There, O'Brien guided them off the trail and in among the trees just as snow began to fall faster.

The forest smelled of rotting wood and worm-rich dirt. It was gloomy but warmer, because the trees offered protection against the sub-zero wind. O'Brien reined in, swung down and busied himself building a small fire and breaking out his battered coffee pot and beans. Charlie slid down off his dun and carefully inspected the animals for any signs of injury or strain. While the water heated, O'Brien sat on a low rock beside the fire and allowed his face to unfreeze. His healing arm was aching and the need for a cigarette was strong in him.

'Not a bad horse you got there, son,' Charlie remarked as he came over and went down on his ankles on the other side of the fire. 'What they call a medicine hat, case you didn't know. Them dapples here, on his legs an' chest. Indians, they set a lot o' store by sich markin's. Say they bring the rider good luck.'

O'Brien pulled off his gloves in order to roll himself a cigarette. 'That's handy,' he replied without looking up. ''Cause on this trip, I reckon we'll need all the luck we can get.'

He offered the makings to Charlie, but the old man shook his head. 'I'm a chewin' man myself,' he replied, rummaging in his jacket pocket for a wedge of molasses-cured, from which he then used his knife to shave off a cud. 'Anyways, iffen you was so damn sure this job couldn't be done, why'd you change your mind an' come along? Nobody twisted your arm, you know.'

'Just plain stupid, I guess.'

'Now, of all the things I might believe you *are*, son, stupid isn't one of 'em.'

'Curious, then. I want to see how you pull this off, granpaw. Six adults, nine children. Two sick and one snow blind that we know of. And between them and safety, a hundred miles of rough country and rougher conditions.'

Charlie grunted and chewed on his cud, working his toothless gums hard to soften the block of tobacco. 'Watch an' learn, boy. Watch an' learn.'

When the coffee started to bubble, O'Brien poured two cups and they sat relishing the warmth and taste with only the hiss of snow falling out on the trail and the occasional snort and stamp of the tethered animals to disturb them. In due course Charlie tossed his dregs onto the fire, rose and stumbled over to the mules, where he checked their loads before they moved on again.

'I calculate we got another three hours' light, iffen we're lucky,' he said, breathing hard now as the combination of chill and altitude went to work on his lungs. 'Might as well make the most of it, 'cause we sure can't risk movin' on after dark, not in this.'

O'Brien nodded and stamped out the rest of the fire, then carried the emptied pot and mugs back to his saddlebags. A few minutes later they emerged back onto the trail and continued their slow, dogged progress ever eastward.

The trail rose steadily up the hillside in an uncertain line that bisected the timber like a streak of iced lightning. About two hundred yards further on, it lifted abruptly, narrowed down and veered to the south and east. To the south the firs cut back to reveal a broad sweep of open ground, spattered with snowy brush and scrub. To the north, a great shoulder of granite shelved up sixty feet high and extended for better than a hundred yards, its serrated rim crowned by stunted juniper, more scrub and large oval boulders.

The afternoon had turned bleaker and colder. Snowflakes fell aimlessly to earth. O'Brien's breathing sounded loud in his ears, and his face began to numb again under the wind's spiteful lash. For just a moment his thoughts turned to the relative warmth and comfort of Scot's Post, and that made the prospect of another two weeks, minimum, in this inhospitable high country even harder to bear.

In fact, he was thinking that when someone took a shot at him.

The deep, deadly crack of a rifle; the whistle and zip of a bullet cutting air north to south, right in front of your face; the receding echo of the shot —

Surprise lasted for all of three seconds. Then O'Brien yanked on the reins and yelled, 'Get off the trail, Charlie! Quick!'

Protesting, the mustang swung around, blundered down off the trail, fell into a deep pocket of snow, heaved back up and kept going down across the open ground, away from the gunfire. Another rifle-shot followed them as they ploughed on, searching for cover, the old man yelling and swearing, O'Brien twisting at the waist, grabbing for the Winchester, sliding the long gun free —

A deadfall loomed up, with a thin cluster of cedar beyond it. Another flurry of bullets snapped through the rarefied air and punched snow-covered bark out of the fallen timber. Without breaking stride, O'Brien sent the mustang up, over the punky wood. The horse cleared it easily, snow trailing from its hooves in a silver-white spray, came down, slipped, regained his balance —

O'Brien threw himself out of the saddle, reins clasped in one hand, Winchester in the other. His horse, spooked by the gunfire, tried to fight him and pull away, but O'Brien held him fast, teeth clenched with the effort, knowing he must secure the animal before he did anything else, lest it bolt and leave him afoot.

He dragged the horse, slipping and sliding, into the cedars, quickly tied him to a low, sturdy branch, then turned and worked the Winchester's action as he came back at a run. Charlie came jouncing up just as he threw himself down behind the deadfall, the mules trotting indignantly in his wake, pack-trees shaking and bouncing on their gray backs. The old man tooled his dun around the deadfall, headed straight for the trees —

More gunfire from the rim of the granite slope now sixty yards away, muzzle-flashes showing bright in the overcast. O'Brien heard lead *thwack* into the wood on the far side of the deadfall, saw it spray snow everywhere.

He came up over the fallen log, slapped the Winchester to his cheek, aimed hurriedly and by instinct, then squeezed the trigger. The rifle spoke with a roar, and O'Brien felt the recoil travel right up to his shoulder. He levered, fired again, then did it all once more, just for luck.

The ambushers — there was definitely more than one of them — blasted back with even greater ferocity than before, or at least that's how it seemed. O'Brien ducked back out of sight as lead crowded the air.

Midway through the volley, Charlie came shuffling out of the trees, long-barreled Dragoon weighing down one skeletal hand, to hit the snow beside him. After that it suddenly went quiet . . . ominously quiet.

The only sound was the old man's labored breathing. O'Brien looked over at him. Charlie's face was bloodless, his green eyes dim, edged with sore-looking rims.

He asked tightly, 'You all right, granpaw?'

Charlie nodded quickly, almost as if he were trying to convince himself. 'Who — ?'

'Can't you guess?'

The old man's bony face hardened. 'Bragg?' he whispered.

'Who else?'

Charlie considered that and chanced a cautious peek over the log. Immediately two rifle-shots flared out of the rocks at the top of the distant slope, chewing up splinters and making the old man drop back out of sight.

'Sonofabitch!' he yelled.

He pushed himself back up almost at once, heedless of his own safety, and cocked and fired the Dragoon. The big black gun twitched in his fist as flame and powder smoke burst from the barrel. O'Brien came up right beside him, aiming for the ambushers' muzzle-flashes, firing, levering, firing again.

For a long moment the high country trembled to the bang and roar of gunfire. Then everything fell quiet again.

'Damn them backshootin' sons-abitches!' Charlie raged bitterly. 'I'll fix their damn flints fer 'em, you jus' — uhn — '

For the second time that day the old-timer hunched up and grabbed himself. O'Brien reached out, put a hand on his arm. Charlie's face was screwed up, his toothless mouth yanked down in a grimace.

'They hit you, Charlie?'

Charlie didn't reply straight away, he couldn't. Then the seizure or whatever it was released its hold on him a little and he shook his head. Another fusillade from the granite ridge peppered the log some more, and they both cringed. As the echoes drifted away, Charlie found his voice again. It was low, husky, weakened.

''M . . . fine . . . All this . . . commotion . . . not good for an' old feller like . . . me.'

O'Brien chanced another look over the deadfall, his rugged face grim. The situation, he knew, was not good. Bragg — as he'd said, who else could it be? — had them pinned down and hugging the only sparse cover available. He could keep them right where he wanted them for as long as he cared to. Or he could send his cousins, Tom and Aaron Quinn, and Rafael da Silva, out to circle around and come at them from behind . . .

Charlie, still breathing hard and ashen-faced, but otherwise pretty much recovered, was thinking along the same lines, his watery eyes now scouring the surrounding country.

'You got any bright ideas, son?' he asked.

'I'm working on it.'

'Be nice if we c'd rout 'em,' the old man mused, scratching thoughtfully at his whiskers. 'Flush 'em outta them rocks.'

It fell quiet again. Wind-driven snowflakes pattered slowly against the brims of their hats and melted against their warm gun barrels. Behind them the horses nickered impatiently, and one of the mules added his voice with a plaintive honk. Suddenly Charlie moved, pushing up onto his hands and knees.

'Where the hell do you think *you're* going?' hissed O'Brien.

'I got me an idea,' the old man announced, turning around to head back to the cedars. 'You jus' keep that fancy rifle o' yourn at the ready.'

'Hold up a minute. Don't you think you ought to tell me what it is you're going to do, first?'

Charlie's face was bleak. 'You'll find out soon enough.'

'Granpaw — '

But Charlie was already gone,

crouch-running back to the trees with another volley of bullets slamming into the deadfall and spitting up snow at his heels.

O'Brien faced front again and threw another couple of shots back at the ridge, knowing that their assailants were too well hidden up there for him to do much more than keep their heads down, and hating the feeling of impotence that came with the knowledge.

All at once it fell quiet again, just the wind, the pattering of snow, the shift and whinny of cold, scared animals.

Then —

'Yee-hahhh!'

O'Brien rolled onto his side just as Charlie's dun exploded from the cedars, with Charlie himself bouncing crazily in the saddle and waving his gun wildly in his fist.

'What — ?'

The old man reined in and the dun went up on its hind legs, fore hoofs pawing the air. 'Watch an old man piss vinegar, son!' he bellowed. '*This'll* flush 'em out!'

He heeled the horse in the flanks and it took off at a gallop, chewing up snow, the old man yawing back and forth in the saddle, hurling insults at the hidden bushwhackers.

'Come on then, you motherless, fatherless, dog-kickin' 'scuses fer men! Come an' see ol' Charlie whip his weight in wildcats!'

The horse thundered on across the open ground with the old man continuing to scream taunts and cuss words. For some timeless moments there was no opposition. Clearly Charlie was doing the last thing anyone had expected, and the shock was immobilizing them.

Until —

The moment ended. Abruptly. And all at once the far ridge came back to life with the rattle of gunfire . . . *all of it aimed directly at Charlie Button.*

4

No longer the immediate target of the bushwhackers, O'Brien came up into a half-crouch and breathed, 'Dammit!'

Recklessly, Charlie kept his mount racing towards the ridge, yelling himself hoarse, cocking and blasting the Dragoon as he went, the dun's flailing hooves all but lost in the snow exploding up around them.

The old man's horse floundered back up onto the trail, kept going straight over to the far side and then up the incline, aiming directly for the spot at which the ambushers had gathered.

Every muscle locked with tension, O'Brien watched the spectacle with the air trapped in his throat. *You crazy old goat, you're gonna get yourself killed —*

It couldn't end any other way, it *couldn't.* Charlie was moving fast, sure, and the snow was helping to make him a harder target to hit, but his luck couldn't hold out forever —

Then — movement. A high, panicky yell that echoed through the stormy afternoon.

O'Brien figured he'd been an onlooker for long enough. He brought the Winchester up as a hat appeared above the scrub, followed by a head, shoulders, torso —

He snap-aimed and fired. Muzzle-flash, roar, recoil — and then the man kind of spun away and dropped out of sight. As he levered again, a second man broke cover, a third, fourth. One of them threw a shot at Charlie. How it missed he would never know.

Charlie fired the Dragoon again. He heard a man howl, either in pain or surprise. Then the old mountain man was right in among them, still yelling obscenities to keep them off balance, horse turning in tight circles, Dragoon spitting thunder and lightning, and God Almighty, they really *were* breaking up before him, turning, making a run for it —

O'Brien twisted around and slip-ran to the trees, untethered his horse and leapt up into the saddle, jamming the Winchester back into leather as he shook out the bridle.

He turned the mustang around and lit out, pulling his handgun now, the handgun being better for close work. He came galloping out of the trees, bent over the mustang's flying mane, Colt in hand, pushed forward, mouth set, eyes slitted, snow slapping him in the face, wind pulling at his hat brim.

Another gunshot, from their attackers up on the ridge, but O'Brien paid it no mind. It was rushed, without aim, the kind of shot you loose off when you're retreating and you're desperate to stop your opponent from coming after you.

Then Bragg and his tag-alongs were gone, out of sight beyond the ridge, and Charlie was gone too, charging after them even though his gun was now clicking on empty.

O'Brien crossed the open ground at a hard run, went across the trail, horse's hooves beating the snow to slush, then up, over the granite slope, gun still at the ready —

The horse bunched its muscles, then leapt the first of the rocks. O'Brien's hat flew off, and went cartwheeling back the way they'd come. Into the timber then. Hoof beats muffled, the sounds of bit and harness mingling with another flurry of gunshots, men yelling —

The ridge sloped down into a snowy clearing before more tall firs crowded together into another belt of timber. O'Brien reined in, legs stiff in the stirrups, raised himself up, looked around —

The firecracker sound of another exchange of lead told him where to go; he jammed his heels into the mustang's wet flanks and they made a mad descent into the clearing, the horse virtually slithering the entire way on his rump. At the bottom they angled northwest, into the next blockade of timber.

Almost at once O'Brien came upon Charlie's horse, standing slantwise across his path, made fidgety and frisky by the run, and Charlie himself down on his knees, chin on his chest, shoulders heaving, one white hand clutching the reins to keep the dun from running.

The drum of hoof beats, moving away at speed. O'Brien's head snapped up, he saw a blur of movement a few hundred yards away, on the other side of the bosque, four riders pushing their horses hard for the west.

Charlie groaned.

O'Brien stepped down fast, leaving his mustang ground-hitched, and hurried across to him, slipping the Colt away. He knelt beside the old man, laid a gentle hand on his back.

Charlie husked, ''M I still . . . alive . . . son?'

'Uh-huh.'

The old man groaned.

'They hit you, Charlie?'

Charlie shook his head. 'Naw . . . Jus' gettin' old . . . old an' . . . wind-broke.' He raised his head slowly. They gone?'

'Uh-huh.'

'I think I hit one of 'em.'

'Me too.'

'Damn cowards.' He spat.

With a wince, he made a move to rise to his feet, and relieved, O'Brien got an arm around his shoulders and helped him up. The old man leaned against his restive horse a moment, very serious, then worked his way along the animal until he came to his saddlebag. O'Brien watched him lift the flap, withdraw the bottle, take a pull, shudder. Now that it was over, he felt a conflict of emotions, and put them into words.

'That was a damn-fool thing you did, you crazy old goat! You could've gotten yourself killed!'

Charlie's tired smile was a taunt. 'I didn't, though, did I?'

'That's not the point.'

'Naw, you're right. The point is that I routed them there Braggs, an' in no uncertain terms. Gave you a good clear shot at one of 'em, nicked another one my own self.'

O'Brien waved that aside. 'The point is that you came all the way up here to fetch a pack of greenhorns out of these hills,' he snapped. 'Not to get your damn self killed.'

Charlie's gummy smile was more of a sneer now. 'Why, son,' he said sweetly, having apparently recovered his wind again, 'I didn't know you cared.'

'I don't,' O'Brien growled, stalking back across to his horse. 'But if anything happens to you, those green-horns become *my* problem.'

Charlie nodded, his eyes glazing a little under the bottle's influence. 'Aw. So ol' Charlie's good fer somethin' then, huh?'

'Just get back on your damn horse and let's get out of here,' O'Brien replied irritably. 'I doubt Bragg'll come after us again. If he's got any sense, he'll tend his wounded and then get back to town while he still can. But the sooner we put some distance between us, the happier I'll feel.'

Charlie put his bottle away and remounted ponderously. 'You . . . sure are a miserable cuss, ain't you?' he remarked.

'If I am, it's you that brings it out in me, granpaw.'

'Aw now, come on, junior. Crack a smile fer ol' granpaw.'

'Shut up, you old buzzard. And stay shut up. You're not the only one who likes to ride in silence, you know!'

They retraced their steps, retrieved O'Brien's hat and then went to collect the tethered mules. The snow eased up again and early darkness filtered down through the dirty clouds.

As the afternoon wound towards evening, they trekked on through timber, across rock-bottomed streams, up gentle grades and down into cups of tree-fringed snow. There was no further trouble.

They rode in silence, except for once when O'Brien took his eyes off the white-green hills ahead to look at his companion and ask, 'Is this the only trail up here from town?'

Charlie eyed him sidelong, head sunk into his shoulders. 'Aw, we're speakin' again, are we? 'M fergiven, am I?'

'Just answer the question, you ornery old buzzard,' O'Brien replied without malice.

Charlie did. 'No, it's not the only trail, but it's the best.'

'You know another?'

'Sure. A few. But not as good.'

'Well, there's no help for that. Starting tomorrow, we'd better travel a less obvious route.'

Charlie gaped at him, then allowed his expression to settle. 'You still thinkin' o' them Braggs?' he grunted.

'They knew the route we'd be taking even before we left town. They got up here ahead of us and just waited for us to show ourselves. That kind of carelessness nearly got us killed.'

Charlie itched at his beard. 'Awright, son. 'Nother trail tomorrow.'

At last the old-timer pointed out a shallow cave in a vast upthrust of rock and by mutual consent they decided to camp there for the coming night. As darkness fell, Charlie checked on the animals while O'Brien crushed and boiled coffee beans and fried bacon steaks cut from a slab of salt hog Peter McGovern had put in with their supplies.

The night was cold and dark, the stars and moon lost behind a blanket of cloud. Finally they settled by the fire to eat, but Charlie only picked at his food.

Watching him, O'Brien said, 'You not hungry?'

The old man pushed the bacon around his tin plate. ''M still tryin' to decide whether or not these here slops is fit fer eatin',' he replied. He paused a moment, then set his plate aside. 'Naw, I don't think they is.'

'Well thanks, granpaw. Maybe you'd like to handle the cooking next time, while I see to the animals.'

'Naw, you carry on, don't fret none about me. I don't eat so much anymore, anyway.' He pushed himself up off his blanket and said, 'Think I'll clean an' trim the mules' feet 'fore I turn in.'

Ravenous himself, O'Brien finished eating, then turned to a chore of his own — checking the ammunition in his handgun and rifle, weapons belt and war bag, shaking each cartridge in turn to make sure that the powder was loose and thus still dry, then wiping each shell with a square of rag to take off any excess moisture.

Behind him, Charlie used a Barlow knife to clean out the horny, elastic soles of the mules' feet, then rasped and shaped the hooves with a file he fetched from his saddlebag, the harsh buffing sounds interrupted every so often by the softer slosh of liquid splashing against a bottle-bottom as he helped himself to the occasional nip.

With their chores done, they bedded

down early, but it took O'Brien a long time to fall asleep. He lay in his blankets for better than an hour, listening to the low, lonely whine of the wind, his head turned against his saddle, watching as a stray draught fanned the embers of the dying fire.

A few feet away, Charlie made a low groaning noise, then rolled onto his side, curled up and fell silent once more, save for the odd snort and snore.

How far had they come? he wondered. Twenty miles? Only a fifth of the distance to Klamath Pass and the stranded greenhorns. Maybe they'd do better tomorrow.

The night passed without event. At first light the following morning, O'Brien went to the cave mouth to relieve himself and then just stood there for a while, stamping his feet, blowing vapor from mouth and nostrils, watching the sun struggle to rise behind them and send powder-blue shadows forward from trees and rocks across acre upon acre of unbroken, settled snow.

His face felt sore and wind-burnt, his eyes raw from snow-glare. His left arm was still throbbing faintly. Raising one hand to his chin, he felt the sharp rasp of bristles.

Finally he heard Charlie begin to shift around in his blankets, and turned to get the fire going. Charlie eased up slowly, pulling a bad-taste-in-the-mouth face before rolling out, hawking and spitting, then going to feed the animals. O'Brien watched him dole out a quart of oats to each of the mules and said, 'Better go easy on the feed, Charlie. It's got to last us for the journey back as well, remember.'

Charlie said, 'Tough day ahead for these critters. Best they do it on a full belly.'

O'Brien shrugged. 'You're the boss.'

'Ayuh. An' don't ferget it.'

Overlooking the old man's pithy manner, O'Brien reached for his skillet. 'You worked up an appetite for my cooking yet, granpaw?'

'Coffee is all.'

'Don't you ever get hungry?'

'Don't you ever mind your own business?'

O'Brien cooked up coffee for them both and fried up some beans for himself. After that came the drawn-out business of repacking the mules, who constantly sidestepped every time O'Brien came close with a pack-tree in his arms, and then saddling the horses. At length they were ready to move out again, Charlie leading the mules, O'Brien fetching up the rear, pale blue eyes busy for signs of life in the seemingly lifeless high country.

Charlie was right — it was a tough day. The slopes were gentle but the packed snow dragged at the animals' hooves and made the going slow and painstaking, especially where the trail virtually petered out and the red firs crowded up as if to cordon off the higher peaks.

But at least the weather held, and as they climbed higher, quail, canyon wrens, horned larks and even pheasants wheeled across the vivid blue sky above them.

Men and animals splashed through one stream after another. O'Brien had never seen land that was more abundant with water. The Sierra Nevada was scored with rivers; the Feather, the American, the Stanislaus, Tuolemne, Merced, San Joaquin, Kings, Tule, Kern.

The day passed achingly cold. O'Brien tugged his bandana up over his lower face and ploughed doggedly on. Charlie continued to take frequent nips from his bottle, and when it was empty he flung it carelessly aside, into a snowdrift. Within another half-mile he was dragging a new bottle from his saddlebag, tilting his head back, riding on in an unsteady manner.

O'Brien held his peace for as long as he could, but when Charlie swayed too far one way and nearly fell out of his saddle, he could remain silent no longer. 'Maybe you better go easy on that skull-bender, granpaw.'

Charlie's only response was a muttered something about O'Brien minding his own business, that he would do damn-well *what* he liked, damn-well *when* he liked.

O'Brien made no further comment. It wasn't worth it. You couldn't argue with a man when he was drunk, especially when he was mean-drunk. All he could hope was that Charlie would see sense in his own time and at least cut his drinking down for the duration of their stay in the mountains.

Charlie's dun stumbled once in the heavy drifts. One of the mules fell onto its side and they had to manhandle the braying beast back onto its feet. Towards the middle of the day the wind picked up and dragged a fresh set of swollen gray clouds down from the north. Exhausted by the effort it had taken just to come this far, they spelled themselves and the animals and boiled coffee. Later they moved on, into the teeth of a fresh blizzard, climbing, always climbing, sucking deeper and deeper of the thin air, pushing themselves and their animals to the limit.

Daylight left the sky when it was only four o'clock or thereabouts, and they virtually staggered into some protecting timber to make camp. Charlie said little. He said yes to coffee, no to food, then shuffled off to check on the animals. Pretty soon after that the old man said goodnight and fell into his blankets.

O'Brien sat alone beside the small fire, nursing a cup of coffee, looking out into the darkness and telling himself to cheer up, 'cause this job couldn't last forever.

Charlie groaned and curled up. O'Brien glanced at the rumpled blankets under which he lay, feeling ambivalent towards his companion, liking many things about him, but *disliking* others.

Probably regretting every swig he took now, he told himself, uncharitably. *Probably wishing he'd stuck to coffee and my lousy cooking, and promising himself he'll do just that tomorrow . . . until tomorrow comes.*

Tomorrow came and went, and so did the day after that, and in all respects each was just a copy of the one that preceded it. Every morning they set off just as soon as it grew light enough to travel safely, and then made as much progress as they could before early darkness stalled them again. Eventually it got so that O'Brien could only remember the hours in between as an endless procession of icy wind, scudding clouds, fast-falling snow and constant climbing.

He found himself wondering grimly what they were going to find waiting for them at trail's end.

They pushed on through as many drifts as they felt able and skirted around those that Charlie considered to be impassable. The howling wind made their ears ache and the driving snow blinded them. The cold was debilitating, but still they pushed on, yard after yard, mile after mile, and the jagged summit came slowly closer and closer. At times O'Brien spotted deer, a bear, the tracks of foraging skunks, and twice heard the cries of a marauding bobcat. But of human life he neither saw nor heard a thing.

Charlie drank incessantly. It seemed to O'Brien that he had an endless supply of brown-glass bottles that he would fetch from one saddlebag or the other, systematically empty and then toss carelessly aside. In one afternoon alone, he fell off his horse three times.

And yet there were occasions when he reverted back to the genial, checker-playing oldster he'd been when O'Brien had first met him, and the sudden thaw in his mood somehow made the travelling easier. He would ramble at great length about his youth and early manhood, and once surprised O'Brien with the revelation that he had been married twice, both times to Indian women, one a Crow, the other a Delaware. The first had died in childbirth — the child was born dead as well — and the second had died in the yellow fever epidemic of '78.

While they were on the subject, the old man asked O'Brien if *he* had ever been married. O'Brien told him no, but said he'd come close once, and when he volunteered no further information and Charlie saw his face kind of tighten down at the edges, that was pretty much the end of the conversation.

Yeah, Charlie was all right at times like that. But then a change would come back over him, a scowl would darken his face, and suddenly it was as if he could hardly get back to his bottle quick enough. His mood would sour again and he would turn cantankerous and impatient, as much with himself as anyone.

O'Brien secretly wondered if his companion was beginning to realize he had bitten off more than he could chew.

Then, five days out of Scot's Post, everything finally became clear.

They were picking a cautious path along the comb of a hill, riding single-file, Charlie up ahead, then the mules, then O'Brien, when the old man suddenly raised a bottle-filled hand to signal a halt. It was the middle of a dismal afternoon, cold as a witch's nipple, with more snow threatening. Charlie had been in one of his blacker moods, hunched up in his saddle, silent and maudlin.

Now he scanned the country that stretched before and below them, and shook his shaggy head slowly. The mountains had scrambled into a series of heavily wooded U-and V-shaped valleys. Far beyond them, the land appeared to drop steeply eastward, down to the other side of the Sierra. A few miles ahead, the sun sent bars of weak sunshine down through breaks in the cloud, and ice shimmered and winked off the boughs of pinon pine and aspen.

Tugging down his bandana, the now-bearded O'Brien called, 'What's up?'

Charlie made no move to reply. It

was as if he hadn't even heard the question. He just shook his head again, then dismounted, the contents of his bottle sloshing wetly, Charlie himself staggering a little as he shuffled forward through the snow, leaving his tired dun ground-hitched. He continued to survey the land ahead, still shaking his head slowly.

Behind him, O'Brien shifted his weight in the double-rig. 'Granpaw?'

When he still didn't get a response, he stepped down and waded up past the patient mules and came to stand beside the old man. Wind whipped powdery snow up along the jagged rims further south; in the gloom the spirals looked like ghosts, retreating before daylight could dispel them forever.

'What's the hold-up, granpaw?'

Charlie glanced at him briefly, then away. His face looked haggard, thin, his skin the color of parchment. 'Nothin'.' But he made *nothin'* sound too much like *somethin'* and worse still, like somethin' *bad*.

'What is it, granpaw?' O'Brien persisted more firmly.

Charlie turned away from him, put the bottle to his lips, threw back his head, then cuffed his mouth dry. It was as he was running his sleeve across his face that he said it. Quietly. Quickly.

'I think we're lost.'

O'Brien squinted at his back for a long moment, watched the wind ruffle the old man's long hair beneath his scarf-tied hat. Angrily he said, 'For crissakes, Charlie, what do you mean, we're lost? We're heading in the right direction, ain't we?'

Ignoring him again, the old man ran his eyes slowly from north to south, taking in everything between, searching for landmarks, anything that he might recognize.

O'Brien watched him, remembering all the boasts the old man had made back in Scot's Post and now mentally calling him all the names under the sun, moon and stars combined. But where was the use in getting mad? It was hardly going to help a situation that called for clear and rational thinking.

Quietly he asked, 'How long have you been leading us astray?'

Charlie shrugged. 'A day. An hour. I don't know.' He waved a bony hand at the terrain before them. 'This all looks kinda different to what I remember. The snow, it changes things.'

'If we turn around, can you get us back on course for Klamath Pass?'

Charlie shook his head again, and when he spoke, his voice was a whine, just like the ever-present wind. 'I . . . I don't know. I gotta think . . . try an' remember where I went wrong . . . '

With a curse he raised the bottle back to his lips, but before he could take another drink O'Brien reached out, fastened gloved fingers on his arm and spun him around. Liquid leapt from the bottle-neck and splashed over his sleeve. The bottle itself fell from Charlie's grasp, landed upright and unbroken in the deep snow at his feet.

For a moment then, the old man

glared at O'Brien, fire suddenly fanning to life in his red-rimmed eyes.

'Do us a favor, Charlie,' O'Brien rasped softly. 'Us and them greenhorns both. Do your thinking with a clear head for a change.'

Charlie pulled out of his hold. 'Lay your friggin' hands on me again an' I'll kill you, junior,' he husked.

O'Brien's eyes were flat, a curious opposite to the too-brightness of Charlie's green orbs. 'If you don't get us back on course,' he said, 'you'll kill *all* of us.'

He turned away and took a couple of paces back to his horse. But as Charlie watched him he slowed his pace, stopped and just stood there for a long moment as fresh snow began to filter down from the stormy heavens.

Charlie watched his back, his broad, damp shoulders, almost afraid.

At length O'Brien turned back to face him. His expression was an unreadable stone mask.

Charlie's eyes flickered away from

him, and he gestured to his horse, his manner suddenly more responsive. 'Ayuh, I'll . . . I'll get us back on track, don't you fret — '

O'Brien said in a dead voice, 'That can wait. I want some answers first.'

'Answers?'

'What is it that's ailing you, Charlie?'

Charlie frowned at him. 'Ailin' me? What you jawin' 'bout, son? Make a little sense.'

O'Brien raised the sleeve across which some of Charlie's whiskey had splashed. Except that it *wasn't* whiskey. The odor was unmistakable. He said, 'Come on, Charlie. This is liquid morphine you've been drinking all this time. You've been killing pain. Or trying to.'

Some of the pretence went out of Charlie's face and it became bleak. 'An' I s'pose you wanna know what *kinda* pain?'

O'Brien nodded.

'Wal, it's none o' your damn business.'

'Oh for crissakes, Charlie — '

'Does it really matter that much? I mean, is it so damn important to you?'

O'Brien just stared at him as snow fell softly around them.

The old man looked away and said grudgingly, 'Awright. I got a cancer. In my stomach. The morphine helps a little. But the worse it gets, the more I got to drink to dull the pain. Satisfied now?'

O'Brien said, 'It's that far gone?'

Charlie replied soberly, a reservoir of emotions suddenly cracking and shattering the wall of a dam, 'Sometimes it's so bad I wanna take out this Dragoon an' put it in my mouth an' blow my brains out. That's how bad it is, the creepin', crawlin' pain of it. But you know what? I don't do it 'cause I ain't got the guts. I keep thinkin', what if it gets better? I don't b'lieve in miracles or sich, an' even if I did, they's plenty folks out there led a more God-fearin' life than me. But I guess ... you allus *hope*. But in the meantime, I try to work it so that somebody else might do it fer me. I tried to pick a fight with John Bragg, I tackled that damn killer Messican o' his, I charged right into all them blastin' guns an' I took on this crazy business, not so's I c'd he'p them folks of McGovern's, aw, nothin' so noble; just 'cause it might finish me off afore the cancer gets any worse.'

He hawked and spat. 'I do all that,' he snorted, 'but somehow ol' granpaw just keeps livin'. Don't seem like there's any justice to it, somehow.'

O'Brien continued to look through the falling snow at him, feeling anger, sympathy, frustration all in one. 'Why the hell didn't you tell me this before we set out?' he demanded.

'What, an' have you treatin' me like I was some kinda invalid? Or tellin' me I was too sick to come? An' don't say you wouldn't of. You an' folks like you, you're real good at tellin' your elders what they should an' shouldn't be doin'.'

'For crying out loud, Charlie, what else would you expect me to say? You shouldn't be chasing around up here in your condition, you ought to be taking it easy back in town, making the most of — '

Charlie cracked one of his sneering smiles. 'Makin' the most'a what's left o' my life?' he finished. 'Hell with that! Now come on, let's get these critters turned around. We gotta go back an' find out where we went wrong . . . '

O'Brien went over to him, bent, picked up his fallen bottle and pressed it back into his hands. He said, 'I'm sorry, Charlie.' And he had never meant anything more sincerely in his entire life.

Charlie clapped him on the arm — his good arm, as luck would have it. 'So'm I, son,' he replied. 'Now come on, let's quit jawin' an' git movin'. Ol' granpaw's got a trail to find!'

5

They plunged back through the now-driving snow with the wind pushing at their rumps, Charlie swilling from the bottle and O'Brien feeling guilty for having prejudged the old man so harshly. Two hours later, Charlie called a halt, hipped around, surveyed their surroundings and then bobbed his head.

'Ayuh. See where I made my error now,' he called back. 'We sh'd be all right from here on down.'

'You sure this time, granpaw? I still haven't forgiven you for the last time yet.'

'Hell, show a little faith ever' once in a while, junior.'

They pressed on, riding northeast now, down through a narrow defile, on into an ice-carved valley, until another stretch of timber heralded the start of the steepest descent yet.

Sitting their horses side by side, Charlie gestured to the land ahead with his bottle. 'It'll be a harder climb down, the slopes on this side bein' that much more preecipitous,' he explained, 'but there won't be so many obstacles in our way, neither. It's more brush than timber.'

He eyed the overcast sky. 'We'll make the journey down tomorrow,' he decided. 'Then, 'bout ten miles further east, that trail yonder feeds right into Klamath Pass. After that, we'll see 'bout gettin' them greenhorns back to safety.'

They found a sheltered spot among tall firs and made camp. After they completed their respective chores, the evening passed slowly, the high-country silence broken only by the singing wind. As O'Brien was just rolling into his blankets, Charlie held out his empty mug and said, 'Much as it grieves me to say it, I reckon I c'd just 'bout stand another cup o' your coffee, son.'

O'Brien looked at him, sensing that

he was being tested in some way. Without stirring, he replied, Tot's right there in front of you, granpaw. Help yourself.'

Charlie shook his head in disgust. 'That's a real Christian attitude you got there, junior,' he noted sarcastically.

'Listen, you old goat. You might be sick, but I'm damn-sure you can still lift a coffee-pot for yourself.'

Charlie muttered something about younger folks having no respect for their betters, and grudgingly refilled his own mug. But five minutes later he muttered, 'Thanks, son.'

O'Brien glanced across at him. In the firelight, the old man's skeletal face was bathed red, his eyes just sunken pits. 'What for? The coffee?'

'Naw. Fer not pamperin' a frail ol' man.'

With elaborate disregard for Charlie's uncharacteristic show of sentiment, O'Brien said, 'Now don't start being nice to me, whatever you do. Just finish your coffee and get some sleep.

Providing you haven't got us lost again, we've got a big day ahead of us tomorrow.'

'Ayuh, that we have.'

A moment of quiet followed. Then: 'Night, granpaw.'

'G'night, son.' They slept.

Along towards dawn, mist wreathed its icy tendrils through the forest and hovered just above the hard ground like wet smoke. O'Brien woke suddenly and with a headache. When he sat up, mist burst gently and bracingly against his face. He rolled out, yawned and shivered, then got a fire started and put water and crushed beans on to heat through.

Silence blanketed the land as he went over to check on the animals. He stiffened suddenly as a shiver ran through the underbrush beside the stacked supplies, then relaxed as he spotted a couple of plundering badgers scurrying away.

Smiling, he looked up beyond the tangled canopy of branches above and studied what he could see of the sky. It was heavy and gray, the clouds appearing to boil as the wind hurried them westward.

Hunkering beside the fire, he rolled and lit a cigarette, then extended his palms towards the flickering warmth and turned his thoughts to McGovern's stranded folks. How well had they survived the last two weeks, he wondered ... supposing they had survived them at all? Had he and Charlie come all this way on a fools' errand, just to find a scattering of frozen bodies awaiting their arrival?

God, he hoped not.

Again he wondered what they were going to find up ahead.

Slowly the dawn light grew stronger and the mist began to sink into the ground. The water in the pot before him made low, plopping noises and O'Brien came up off his ankles, threw down his butt and turned toward Charlie's sleeping form.

'Come on, granpaw, stir yourself.

We're burning daylight.'

He reached down for their cups, held them both in one hand and picked up the coffee-pot with the other.

Charlie didn't move.

O'Brien glanced around at him again, a frown in his voice. 'Charlie?'

There was no response.

He put the cups down, set the pot onto a stone at the edge of the fire, went over to the old man.

'Charlie?'

He knelt beside the blanket-draped figure, gently tugged back one edge of the cloth to study the old man's face. Fearing the worst then, he put a palm against Charlie's face — cold — reached under the blanket, pulled the old man's jacket open, searched for heartbeat or pulse.

His voice dropped to a whisper.

'Ah, Charlie.'

Charlie was stretched out on his back, head braced on his saddle, eyes shut, mouth shut, perfectly at rest.

Charlie was dead.

Shaken, O'Brien covered him back up and rose slowly to his full height, numbed by shock, stunned by the speed with which it had happened. *Charlie, Charlie, after all this . . . after you came all this way . . .* He shook his head, baffled by the whims of Fate, a part of his brain still unable to accept what every other sense was telling him, angry that the old man's life should have come to this, sad for him, glad for him, and suddenly awesomely, completely *alone*.

Alone, that was, but for the greenhorns he — no, *Charlie* — had come out here to rescue.

Suddenly O'Brien's voice was heavy with responsibility. 'Aw, Christ.'

His head seemed to throb harder. He went back to the fire, bent, poured coffee into one mug and drank it down while it was still scalding, not feeling it, too busy thinking about the wider implications of Charlie's death now, about where it left *him*, O'Brien, about the impossible mission he had suddenly inherited.

Again he muttered, 'Aw, Christ.'

What the *hell* was he going to do now?

The answer to that was simple, of course. He was going to see it through.

Not because he owed it to McGovern, or Charlie, or McGovern's folks, though that would have made for a good story. No. Purely and simply because he had no choice. Like it or not, he was stuck with it.

He drank down another cup of coffee, smoked another cigarette, his tactician's brain already going back to work, preparing him for what still lay ahead in Klamath Pass. Finally he threw the butt into the fire, went back over to Charlie and looked around.

Here was as good a place as any to bury the old man, he supposed, and perhaps it was a better place than most, given that Charlie had spent so much of his life in the high country. But though McGovern had packed a couple of shovels in with the rest of their gear, the ground was too frozen to dig easily.

Never mind. There was a way around that.

O'Brien smartened the old man up as best he could, brushed out his beard, straightened out his clothes, then went through his few personal possessions and put a couple of bits and pieces in with him before he wrapped him in a blanket, then a tarp, and fastened the whole lot into a kind of cocoon with rope. He found a good spot under a sturdy Douglas fir on the far side of camp and laid the body out beneath it, then went in search of rocks, and as dawn turned into early morning, he fashioned a cairn over the body that would, in the end, keep out all but the biggest and most persistent predator.

When he finished, he searched his mind for a prayer, something pretty, but since he couldn't think of one, and since Charlie had told him he'd never been a God-fearing man anyway, he made do with just a simple two-word epitaph.

'Goodbye, granpaw.'

He stood before the rock mound, head bowed, hands fisted at his sides. The moment was solemn, silent. Behind him, one of the horses nickered and stamped.

And in the very next moment —

A shot rang out and a bullet spanged off the cairn, splintering rock, sending shards everywhere.

O'Brien thought, *What the hell* — Then he twisted around and down, caught a blur of movement as he went, a man, racing left to right through the trees sixty feet away, long hair flying, arms pumping, shadows spilling back off his head and shoulders —

A yell; another; another; more a series of war-cries really, and more movement — but by then O'Brien had seen enough. All at once there was no time for anything but action.

As they crashed out of the surrounding trees and came dashing across the campsite towards him, he did some running of his own, over to his gear.

He threw himself at his saddle, went down, closed his hands on the stock of his Winchester, and the rifle whispered from leather and went with him. He rolled, came up on one knee, worked the action, aimed at the man in the lead and fired at him.

The first bullet hit him in the chest and shattered his sternum. O'Brien saw blood streak from the wound and quickly shot him again. That time the bullet hit him a little higher and to the right, and blood squirted there, too; then the man buckled, twisted, dropped his own weapon — an old Springfield .45/70 — and collapsed in a heap.

An arrow sliced through the air, turning fast. O'Brien heard it flash past, strike the cairn behind him, shatter. He jacked in another shell and turned the Winchester onto a shorter, squatter man, coming at him from the left. Dimly it registered with him that there were five of them — four now — and that they were Indians, possibly Utes or Shoshones.

This bastard rushed at him like he couldn't wait for the two of them to tangle. O'Brien saw his coppery face yanked out of shape by a wild yell, saw the flash of his dark eyes, the dazzle of his yellow teeth —

He shot the Indian in the face and turned just as the third leapt over Charlie's saddle and rushed at him. They collided and went staggering, both of them winded by the impact and struggling to keep their balance on the slippery ground. Then the Indian tried to brain O'Brien with a club, but O'Brien ducked low and to the side, quickly shot the fourth Indian before he could join the fray and then swung back to the third, using his Winchester as a club now.

He clobbered the Indian in the side of the head and something gray and meaty dribbled out of one of the sonuver's ears before he hit the ground and kicked his last.

That just left —

O'Brien saw the fifth Indian throw a

heavy-bladed hatchet at him and leapt aside as it turned end over end through the thirty feet of air that separated them and then *thwacked into* a tree-trunk.

Down on his knees, O'Brien swapped a look with the Indian, saw a bronzed, mean-looking face with fierce eyes, a hooked nose, a snarling mouth, the whole thing framed by long, greasy black hair.

Then —

With a cry that echoed through the forest, the Indian dragged a heavy Starr .44 from his belt and tried to shoot O'Brien.

O'Brien shot him first. Twice.

The Indian jerked under the force of the hammering bullets. His dirty buffalo-hide jerkin fairly exploded as the .44/40s hit him, and he went over backwards and stayed there.

O'Brien held his breath for a long beat, locked right where he was, only his eyes moving as he checked on the bodies. One . . . two . . . three . . . four . . . five. One of them wriggling slowly, nearer to death than life, the other four already as stiff as statues.

At last the fifth Indian groaned his last and died. O'Brien released his breath and pushed up onto his feet. The horses and mules were tugging at their tie-ropes and side-stepping in agitation, and he couldn't blame them. The sudden explosion of war-cries and gunfire had left him temporarily deafened, and when he looked at all the blood that was splashed across the snow, blood that was melting its way *into* the snow because it was still warm, he felt kind of agitated himself.

Slowly his heart stopped its hammering, his belly stopped rolling, his pulses calmed, and he thought, *On top of everything else, what the hell's this all about?*

He worked the lever again, just in case there were any more of them out in the forest, but common sense told him that they would've made their presence known by now.

Even so, it wasn't a good idea to hang

around any longer than he could help. He had to put some distance between him and this place.

Briefly he checked on the dead men. But after the first two his grimace turned to a frown, because they weren't like any Indians he'd ever seen before. A closer examination told him that they weren't Utes or Shoshones, as he'd thought, but instead a hybrid mixture of the two. Their clothing was a mixture, too; part red man's buckskins, moccasins and painted, quilled leggings, part white man's boots, shirts and hats, all of it threadbare, run-down, some still stained by the blood of the dead men it had been stolen from.

O'Brien ran his eyes across their discarded weaponry. It ranged from stone-age clubs and crude bows to ancient cap-and-ball pistols and a no-doubt pilfered Army-issue Springfield rifle, everything in poor condition.

He knelt beside one of the bodies and tried to put everything together so that it made sense. In the end there could only be one answer; that these miserable remnants were Digger Indians — one of many different outcast and degenerate sub-cultures of the various Indian tribes. Many of those who occupied the Sierra Nevada — the Miwoks, Yokuts and the Salinan — were peace-loving, shy, religious after a fashion, and kept to themselves as best they were able. But others, like this band of Ute-Shoshone mongrels, were warlike, savage, greedy and completely without honor. It was only his good fortune that they had launched their attack on impulse. If they'd formulated a plan of action first . . . But that wasn't their way, they didn't have the patience or discipline for that.

He glanced at Charlie's grave. It was hard to believe that the old man was really dead, and the absolute certainty of it drove a spike into his belly.

He saddled the horses — you never knew, he might need Charlie's dun — and got the mules loaded, then fastened the dun's reins to the second mule's tail and led them east, out of the forest. The dun balked at first. It didn't want to leave Charlie behind. But after a while, the old horse settled down and gave no more trouble.

O'Brien stayed alert, with the now-reloaded Winchester propped against his leg, ready for use. He rode that way until the timber fell behind them and the steep, hazardous descent lay ahead.

'Whoa, boy.'

The wooded incline dropped about a thousand feet into a broad, long valley, and he wanted to study it carefully before they started down. Mist still lingered along the valley bottom, gray and diaphanous, with evergreens and scrub oak projecting from its murky depths, alongside manzanita, sage and bitterbrush.

He took a battered pair of field glasses from one saddlebag and ran them over as much of the country as he could see, just in case there were any more Diggers loitering in the vicinity, but the high country seemed as devoid of life as it had before.

As he put the glasses away, however, the heavy clouds to the north suddenly broke and weak sunshine fanned its shimmering rays down onto the vista below. The light caught on something that reflected it like a starburst, and O'Brien actually flinched away from the unexpected brightness until he realized it must be bouncing off the restless waters of the distant Feather River.

At last he shook the bridle out and told the mustang to move on. The horse elected to follow a long, zigzag trail down to the snowy valley floor, and O'Brien allowed him to pick his own pace. The mustang was reluctant to go at first, and his reluctance somehow communicated itself to the other animals. All O'Brien could do was make soothing noises to stop them from losing their nerve completely, and keep them moving slowly along the thin, meandering path until eventually they descended right into the mist itself and after some timeless eternity the valley floor pushed up magically beneath them.

The morning was bitterly, miserably cold, and to make matters worse, it was the kind of cold that seeps through a man's clothes and gets right inside his belly, then stays there no matter how hard he tries to dislodge it. Just the thought of it alone was enough to make O'Brien shiver.

The mustang trudged on, high-stepping through the snow in a curiously dainty fashion, the rest of the animals following docilely along in his wake.

O'Brien's eyes never stayed still beneath the line of his hat, but they met no further opposition as they travelled the wide, empty valley down to the lower, mistier passes.

Again his thoughts turned to Charlie. At last the old man had gotten what he wanted — release from his pain. And for that, O'Brien was glad. But there was no doubting that Charlie's death had left him in a pretty fix.

It started snowing again, and he huddled lower in his saddle and had to heel the mustang in the flanks to keep him going. For better than ninety minutes they forged on through the silent valley, past stunted, snow-capped juniper and aspen, past big, eroded rocks and spindly pinon. And all the time the ground dipped steadily ahead of them, taking them ever lower . . .

At last they reached the far end of the valley and O'Brien hauled in before a gap between two sheer granite escarpments. He had to narrow his eyes against the driving snow by this time, and as the wind howled out of the ravine it unsettled the already-spooked animals, making them prance and toss their heads.

As best he could, O'Brien studied the country ahead. The gap opened out into a winding corridor of rock about two hundred feet across. It extended for about five hundred feet, then turned sharply towards the north, so that anything beyond that point was presently hidden from view. Snow filled the gorge to choking-point, and piled itself higher still along the bases of the walls. Brush sprouted from wherever it had managed to find a foothold in the weathered ramparts, snow-covered and wind-tossed now, and the path ahead was littered with huge, misshapen boulders and the occasional bare, tortured tree.

O'Brien thought, *So this is Klamath Pass*.

He gigged the mustang back to movement and they entered the defile, the horse's steps suddenly increasing in volume, *shu-sha . . . shu-sha . . . shu-sha . . . shu-sha . . .* and knocking back off the high walls as hollow echoes.

The horse stumbled a couple of times as he followed the trail around to the north. Snow rapidly filled in the tracks they left behind them. O'Brien felt anticipation rise within him, anticipation and apprehension both, because whatever he found here now was going to dictate what came next; namely, how they were going to get the hell back over the mountains to Scot's Post.

They swung north, around the bend.

He wasn't sure exactly what it was he was expecting to find, but whatever it was, it wasn't there. All that confronted him was more of the same — a broad, snow-choked pathway hemmed in by high rock walls that stretched on north, right into an overcast sky the color of pencil lead.

Wind buffeted horse and rider. The mustang spooked a little more, trotted and shook his head. O'Brien got him settled down again and kept him going forward, past slopes covered in sage and chaparral and chamiso. *Shu-sha . . . shu-sha . . . shu-sha . . . shu-sha . . .*

A bullet whined out of nowhere and drilled into the snow six feet ahead of them. The horse shied back with a whinny, and O'Brien's head snapped up. He saw the figure of a man sky-lined on the far ridge, long hair blowing crazily in the wind, and fired the Winchester at him one-handed.

The figure quickly dropped out of sight. O'Brien shoved the Winchester into leather and drew his Colt. It looked like he'd been wrong about those Diggers. There *were* more of them around these parts.

The same or another figure poked his head up over the ridge again, and O'Brien threw another bullet at him. A sudden flurry of gunshots came whip-cracking down in reply. One slammed into the tarp-wrapped supplies on the first mule's sturdy back, but fortunately did the mule itself no harm.

All at once snow swirled more violently around them, slicing visibility down to just yards. Taking advantage of it, O'Brien jabbed the horse in the sides and got them moving again.

The presence of the Diggers here at this time worried him. McGovern's folks had enough to contend with as it was, just trying to stay alive, without a bunch of savages harrying them as well.

He fought the mustang on through the pass as wind shrieked down at him from the north and shook more snow loose from the heavens above. He felt like a fish in a barrel in this rocky bottleneck. How long was this damned pass, anyway? Just how far had McGovern's party managed to get before they'd become stranded?

Wind shoved them one more time, and the mustang minced sideways on to it. In the saddle, O'Brien suddenly stiffened and leaned forward. For just a moment there, he thought he'd seen a flash of color up ahead, not the same deadening combination of white, gray and green but *real* color, red.

Without warning he caught sight of it again, some sort of homemade flag, snapping madly in the wind forty yards away, a beacon that was trying to say, *Here we are; now for pity's sake help us!*

Galvanized back into action, he raised the Colt and fired three fast shots into the sky. A moment later a rifle barked back a response — BAM! BAM! BAM! — and he kicked the horse forward, excitement building.

Slowly the flag grew sharper to him. He realized it was a man's shirt, tied by the sleeves to an up-ended wagon tongue. More details leapt out to him then; the shape of the wagon itself . . . two wagons . . . two massive Conestogas brought together to form a protective 'L' up against the east-side wall of the ravine.

And there, peering carefully around the edge of one wagon — a man! Big, bearded, bundled up in an old chesterfield overcoat, and fisting a repeater across his body.

O'Brien tugged down his bandana and yelled, 'Hello the camp! White man coming in!'

The other man's reply was carried to him on the wind. ' . . . come ahead . . . but be . . . real careful now . . . '

He rode nearer, hardly able to believe that he had finally reached his goal.

It was then that he realized that what

he had first taken to be low, snow-covered rocks scattered across the ground between him and the wagons, were in fact dead bodies.

A wild scream suddenly rent the air, and he hipped around quickly. A figure was coming at him from behind an outcrop sixty feet away, covering the distance in a lurching, helter-skelter run; a man, short, stocky, muffled against the cold and wielding a lance.

O'Brien brought his gun up, but the roar of a rifle beat him to it. Snow burst up in front of the Digger but still he came running, running and yelling —

Another rifle-shot crack echoed across the pass. The Digger hunched up, fell backwards and rolled onto his stomach. He writhed for a while like a snake with a broken back, then began to crawl away, leaving his lance, and roses of blood stark against the white of the snow, where they fell.

O'Brien put his eyes back onto the wagons. The big, bearded man was just lowering his smoking rifle, and another man was waving his arms frantically, telling O'Brien not to tarry.

He threw one last look at the Digger, still inching back the way he'd come, then ran his gaze up across the high ridges. It was beginning to look more and more like he really had his work cut out for him this time.

With one eye on his back trail, he led the animals through a gap between the wagons and swung down.

6

All at once he was surrounded. Two women, two men, a bunch of older children, all of them swathed in jackets, blankets or shawls, anything and everything that might help to keep them warm; they all came forward to grab him by the arm, shake him by the hand or just to touch him, to assure themselves that he was real and not a figment of fevered imagination. O'Brien looked from one gaunt, pale face to the next, saw desperation in their dark-ringed eyes, a kind of wild, pitiful hope that only increased the already heavy sense of responsibility within him. They were all babbling at once, firing questions at him, thanking God for answering their prayers, asking him how long it would be before his companions got here. Both the women and a few of the children were sobbing, expelling clouds of vapor into the frosty noon air, hardly able to breathe with emotion.

He let it go on for so long, then raised his hands for quiet. Dutifully they fell silent. One of the men and an older boy-child, about fifteen years of age, went back over to the gap between the wagons, to keep watch on the pass and throw occasional looks back over their shoulders to hear what he had to say.

As wind snapped at wagon canvas and the tarpaulin they'd strung from the hoops of one wagon to the other to give themselves more protection and shelter from the unfriendly elements, O'Brien tried to answer it all in one go.

He told them who he was, how he came to be there, and that he was there alone. He didn't mention Charlie, much as Charlie deserved some recognition. He figured that the greenhorns were demoralized enough as it was; to hear that one of their rescuers had died coming over the mountains — even though his death had had nothing whatever to do with the actual crossing — was hardly likely to inspire the confidence they would need for the long haul back. He explained the old dun away — truthfully, now — as his spare mount.

As he spoke, he saw some of the hope in their eyes flicker and die. He wasn't surprised. It wasn't that they were ungrateful, merely that they'd been expecting/hoping/praying for something more than just one man to come to their rescue.

When he finished, the big, bearded fellow told a couple of the other boys to take the horses and mules away, then ushered O'Brien over to their small fire. Freezing, O'Brien went gratefully, and secure in the knowledge that a bulge in the rock wall overhead would prevent the Diggers from shooting down on them from above.

The boys took the animals to a spot forty feet away, where a patch of ground sheltered by high rocks doubled as a sort of holding pen. O'Brien saw eight oxen standing resolutely in the snow, batting big, stoic eyes against the swirling flakes. Four dead oxen lay nearby, one little more than bone and gristle, another partially butchered for meat.

One of the women looked up and said, 'Please, Mr. O'Brien . . . my son, David . . . Did he m-make it through all right?'

O'Brien nodded. 'He's a brave boy, ma'am. You can be proud of him.'

She sagged and whispered, 'Oh, thank God.'

The big man said keenly, as he and the other two women gathered around him, 'You . . . you fetched supplies? Food? Coffee?'

'As much as McGovern could pack aboard two mules.'

The man turned to the small, lifeless woman who stood next to him and hugged her roughly. Her restless brown eyes clearly identified her as McGovern's sister; she had pulled-back, dark-but-graying hair and a pinched, undernourished face that testified vividly to two tough weeks in the mountains.

'Hear that, Rose?' he said in a tone that was meant to keep their spirits up. 'I knew Peter wouldn't let us down!'

Seeming to shed years with relief, she returned her attention to the man, obviously her husband. 'We . . . we'll see about unloading the mules, then . . . sh-shall we? Come on, Kate.' And together, she and the other woman hurried towards the makeshift holding pen, a bunch of children trailing behind them.

When she was gone, the big man, ragged and aged, introduced himself as Arthur Conway, McGovern's brother-in-law. He was of an age with his wife, about forty, tall and broad, with small, close-set brown eyes and thick hair curling down from under his black, loose-brimmed hat. He gestured to the man who had gone to keep an eye on the pass, introducing him as James Eddings, his late sister's husband.

O'Brien frowned, and Eddings nodded morosely. He was shorter than Conway, about five years younger and a little lighter, with a thin face, a ragged, whiskery chin and sunken, haunted-looking gray eyes. 'Yeah,' he choked. 'Alice, she . . . once the fever took hold of her there was just . . . ' Unable to say more, he just shook his head, reached out and hugged the boy beside him.

Conway sleeved at his own moist eyes. 'We . . . we buried her about three days ago, back there a ways,' he said.

Nodding, O'Brien glanced over his shoulder at the second of the two women, now helping Rose to unload the supplies from the mules. She was tall, gracefully built, somewhere in her late twenties, with long raven-black hair framing an oval face that was dominated by two large well-spaced hazel eyes and small naturally red lips. Realizing that he hadn't introduced her, Conway now said, 'Uh, that's Jimmy's sister, Kate. Fine girl. And a tower of strength to their poor, suffering kids.'

He let his breath out through his nose and shook his head. 'It's been a grievous business, Mr. O'Brien,' he confided in an undertone. 'First Joe Coldeway, our guide, then my poor sister, God rest her — '

O'Brien turned his attention back to the other man. 'Your guide died as well?'

'I tell you, I never met a braver man. Snow blind, he was, but still he fought beside us against them redgut savages, till they split his skull with an axe — '

'What's the story with the Indians, Conway? I ran into a pack of them myself, this morning.'

Conway shook his head again, this time in a combination of bewilderment and despair.

They showed up one night about a week ago, a dozen of 'em. Just crept up and tried to steal our oxen. Well, we couldn't allow that, so there was a fight. We shot a couple of the bastards, and they killed poor Joe. We thought we'd seen the last of them after that; hoped, I guess, but no such luck. Ever since then, they've been trying to pick us off so they can help themselves to what little we've got left.'

'They're Digger Indians, Conway,' O'Brien told him. 'That's what they do. Forage. Take. Steal. Whatever it takes to get what they want, except buy it, work for it or barter. It was most likely the mules and supplies they were after when they took a stab at me.'

'Damn them!' Conway spat. 'We've done well to hold them off as long as we have, I guess, but we can't hold them off forever. We're running low on ammunition for one thing, and for another, it's taking a dreadful toll on the women and children.' He put tortured eyes over O'Brien's ruddy, bearded face, his expression vaguely baffled, quietly horrified. 'I can't tell you how many of them we've already killed,' he whispered, the need for confession weighing heavy on him.

'*Killed*' he repeated for emphasis. 'Lord, do you know how terrible it *is* to kill another man, even a redgut savage?'

Quietly, and with supreme understatement, O'Brien said, 'I know.'

He glanced around the camp. It was cramped, draughty and cluttered. 'Your son mentioned that his aunt and one of her kids was sick. If the child's still poorly, I fetched some medicine with me.' Remembering Charlie, he added, 'Morphine, too.'

Conway shook his head. 'No, the child recovered, though she's still weak and has trouble keeping whatever we feed her down. I guess she had more resistance than ... ' He swallowed audibly.

O'Brien changed tack. 'Then all of your people can be moved?'

'Yes.' Conway studied him closely again. 'But I'm not sure we can risk it. I mean, even if you discount these ... what did you call them? Diggers? Even if you discount those, I don't suppose we'd get too far in these conditions.'

O'Brien had to acknowledge the sorry truth of that, but only to himself. Briefly he reviewed in his mind the journey he'd already made to get here. It had been hard enough on *him*, never mind townsmen, women and children. Apart from which, there were the wagons to consider. They'd never get them up the steep trail he'd descended to reach Klamath Pass.

He said, 'Did your guide have a map, Conway?'

Conway reached into his chesterfield, drew out a thin dog-eared square of rawhide and handed it over. 'I doubt you'll make anything out of it. Joe understood it well enough, but we've studied on it and it means nothing to us.'

O'Brien unfolded the map. It was timeworn and faded, little more than a series of curved or wriggling lines and a rough cross that was meant to signify the points of the compass.

The women came back to the fire, still surrounded by children. In their arms they cradled some of the supplies McGovern had packed for them. O'Brien saw Conway hurriedly banish all the worry and uncertainty from his wind-burnt, peeling face so that his wife would only see a man who apparently knew for a fact that everything was going to be fine.

Rose said, 'Look, Arthur — coffee, some bacon and flour, sweetening and potatoes!'

Her husband put a big hand on one of her small shoulders and said with forced enthusiasm, 'Why, we'll dine like royalty before we leave this place, Rose! Do you hear that, kids?'

It was the crack in his voice that gave him away. Then, so suddenly that it took them all by surprise, his shoulders sagged and his head dropped and all at once he was crying soundlessly at how pitiful all of this seemed, how far he and all his family had fallen in so short a space of time, and when Rose quickly passed the supplies across to her sister-in-law and went to hold him and tell him that was all going to be fine, that was the saddest, most pitiful thing of the lot; the big man crying, the frail, sick-looking woman offering comfort like a mother to a child with a grazed knee.

O'Brien turned away in order to give Conway some small measure of privacy, and went to check on the animals. The big man had just about run out of rope. This business had pushed him, all of them, to the limit. But it wasn't over yet. Getting them out of here in one piece was going to be the hardest part of it all, because as Conway himself had pointed out, if the Diggers didn't get them, the elements would.

His left arm was throbbing again, and shoving the old map into his pocket, he reached up to massage it. Out beyond the stone holding pen, snow was falling steadily. It was only going to make his task more difficult. He thought about the gaunt, ill-looking children, some of them already motherless. About the women. Conway. His brother-in-law, Eddings, now a widower.

Then he thought about the mountains, the weather, the Indians.

His arm started throbbing harder.

He threw his gear into a spare corner, followed it down and, with his back to the rock wall, thought about the predicament in which he now found himself. Rose Conway fetched him a mug of coffee and he nodded his thanks. Then he rolled and lit a cigarette and thought some more while he watched the people he hoped to help go about the business of survival.

Sometime later he saddled the mustang and rode out to take a look at the rest of Klamath Pass. His thinking was that if they couldn't go any further forward, then maybe they could go *back*. Of course, the weather and the Indians might have something to say about that, but at the very least he might be able to marry up a landmark or two to the ancient map and get his bearings a little clearer.

The wind had dropped and it had long since stopped snowing, although the sky was still as gray as gunpowder. He rode cautiously, keeping as near to the east wall as he could so that the Diggers — if they were up there — wouldn't be able to shoot down on him easily.

Klamath Pass extended north for another few miles, then fed out into a vast network of wide-open downward-sloping plains, with Black oak and Ponderosa pine splashing cones of emerald green across an otherwise bleak, white landscape, and thicker timber forming yet another wooden rampart to the north. Again he saw weak, dying daylight sparkling off a distant watercourse through the interlaced trees and branches.

Reining in, he fished out the map and pored over it for a few minutes, alternatively transferring his gaze from the seemingly meaningless hand-drawn lines to the planes and contours of the country that surrounded him. Nothing seemed to match up; leastways nothing that he could see.

He swore under his breath, turned the horse around and rode away.

Full dark was approaching by the time he hailed the camp and walked the mustang in. The women were busying themselves over a steaming pot suspended above a small, smokeless fire, and the promise of thick ox-meat stew carried to him on the bracing early-evening air. James Eddings and his oldest son were sleeping beneath a jumble of blankets, while Conway and another boy were standing watch. A couple of the older girls were looking after the younger children, who were sleeping, reading or playing desultorily.

He swung down, hauled the double-rig off the horse's back and up-ended it nearby, then peeled off the blanket beneath and set about drying the damp animal off as best he could.

Conway called softly to him. Rose and Kate were starting to ladle stew onto plates and pass them around. As O'Brien walked back to the fire, an eleven-year-old girl with a very serious face brought his plate over to him. He thanked her and took it back to the corner he had claimed for himself.

After a long ride through a cold afternoon, the food was welcome, and finally dispelled the headache he'd woken up with earlier that morning. For a time the camp was quiet but for the sounds of adults and children eating, the shift and shake of miserable animals and the low moan of northerly winds. O'Brien thought about the cairn he'd left behind him on the other side of the broad, misty valley, the tarpaulin-wrapped body of Charlie Button and the five hard-frozen Digger Indians he'd killed. Suddenly that place seemed like the loneliest place on earth, lonelier even than this forlorn ravine.

When he finished eating, he set his plate aside and settled down to think some more and refine what was already coalescing in his mind. The women got the children ready for sleep — they all slept around the small fire, partly for warmth and partly because the wagons were primarily used as barricades against the Diggers — and did their best to ease the nighttime fears of the youngest by telling them some old and familiar fairy tales.

O'Brien looked out into the darkness. Moonlight reflecting off snow made the night glow strangely, and shadows took on a depth and life of their own. Distractedly he rubbed at his left arm, which was itching more than throbbing now.

'Are you all right, Mr. O'Brien?'

As buttery light fell across him, he glanced up to find Kate Eddings coming over with an oil-lamp held high in one hand. Startled, he said quickly, 'Best you douse that lamp, ma'am. There's Diggers out there, don't forget.'

Instead, she set the lantern down on a low rock and sat opposite him, carefully arranging her long, heavy coat around her. The lamplight threw dark gold across her alabaster skin and lit fires in her wide hazel eyes. 'It's all right. Apart from that first night, the Indians haven't bothered us much after dark, though we still keep a watch, just in case.'

'You should. That's the thing about Diggers — you never know which way they'll jump next.'

She eyed him carefully. 'Are you all right?'

He nodded. 'Yes, ma'am. I've got some stitches in my arm that are just about ready to come out, that's all.'

'Stitches?'

'I had a little, uh, accident about a week ago. Cut myself.'

'Is there anything I can do to help?'

'It'll keep.'

'Are you sure? From the sound of it, you'd be better off if they came out now.'

'I can see to it, ma'am,' he replied. Something suddenly occurred to him and he smiled gently. 'And when I do, I guess you could say it'll be a case of 'suture self'.'

Either it wasn't funny to start with or, more likely, this was neither the time nor the place to try and raise the spirits with a show of levity, because her face remained serious. 'Here,' she said. 'Take your jacket off and roll up your shirt sleeve while I go and fetch a knife.'

'I've already got a knife,' he replied. 'But with respect, ma'am, cutting and pulling stitches isn't my idea of woman's work.'

Her expression withered him. 'You might be surprised at what women are capable of,' she said.

His mouth moved into another easy smile as he told her sincerely, 'Ma'am — *nothing* would surprise me where women are concerned.'

'Is that a good thing, or a bad one?'

'It's meant well.'

'Then let's have no more of this shilly-shallying,' she said, holding out one small, gloved hand. 'The knife, if you please.'

He could see there was going to be no arguing with her, so he resignedly handed over his old jack-knife and then unbuttoned his jacket and drew out his left arm. At once he shivered. They'd better make this quick. He rolled up his shirtsleeve, revealing the closed, faintly pink scar and the ugly-looking black stitches that clamped it. He watched her face, waiting to see some sign of revulsion or reluctance to even touch them, but her expression remained neutral; she took his arm in one hand, tilted it towards the lamplight, then set to work.

'Tell me if it hurts,' she muttered.

'I will, ma'am, don't you fret about that.'

She made short work of it, although she didn't rush, and it only hurt a bit. One by one the stitches came free and she drew them out and cast them aside.

'You are used to pain, Mr. O'Brien?' she inquired. 'You bear it silently and with dignity, if I may say so.'

'Well — uh — I'm not sure I'd agree

with you on — uh — *that*, but . . . I guess you learn to take a few knocks in my line. You *have* to.'

She frowned. 'What exactly *is* your line?'

'Trouble,' he replied softly.

She looked sharply at him, then went back to her work. 'I hope that means you *deal* with trouble, Mr. O'Brien, and not *make* it.'

'I'd like to think so, ma'am.'

Finally she said, 'There — it's done.'

He rolled his sleeve down and quickly shucked back into the sheepskin, already chilled to the bone. 'Obliged to you, ma'am.'

She gave him his knife back. 'It is we who are obliged to you, Mr. O'Brien,' she said.

'I haven't done anything for you yet.'

She disagreed. 'You risked your life to come this far,' she argued. 'You brought supplies for us. You will be getting us away from this wretched place.' She looked at him more carefully then, and asked softly, 'You *will*, won't you?'

He looked back at her, not speaking, trying to reach a decision. At last he said, 'Let's go talk to the rest of your folks.'

He climbed to his feet, helped her up, picked up the lamp and escorted her back to the fire.

The camp was quiet but for the sounds of children sleeping and stirring under thick gray blankets, and Rose looked up from cradling one sleeping baby as they came into the ring of firelight.

O'Brien said, 'All right, listen up.'

Conway and the other boy turned their faces towards him, and James Eddings sat up and knuckled his sunken eyes. O'Brien sucked down a draught of bitter air and said, 'We're pulling out, just before sun-up tomorrow.'

Absolute silence greeted his statement. Then Eddings got up and brushed himself down. His short black hair was rumpled and his haggard, whiskery face was puffed from sleep.

'You've got a plan?' he croaked, clearing his throat after he spoke the final word, and jamming his old gray hat on to keep his head warm.

O'Brien held back from replying at once, unwilling to commit himself completely, but then nodded. 'Yep, I've got a plan, and I'll be honest with you, it's a chancy one. But no more chancy than staying right here and waiting for the Diggers to come and lift your scalps.'

Rose stood up, the baby still held in her arms. Her intake of breath was sharp, and Conway came over to put an arm around her shoulders. Kate, meanwhile, went to stand beside her brother, so that in the end they were all lined up facing him.

Kate said, 'Well . . . what *is* the plan?'

He sketched it out briefly. There wasn't time to go through the whole thing in more detail — if truth be told, he didn't have all the details worked out anyway. He said, 'We can't go forward. There's no telling how many Diggers might be waiting for us up ahead. But we *can* go back.'

Conway's mouth worked for a moment before he said, 'Back? Over all the ground we've already covered?'

'Not all of it.'

Eddings said, 'But who's to say the Indians won't pursue us?'

O'Brien looked at him. 'I plan to buy the Indians *off* Mr. Eddings.'

Kate breathed, 'What?'

He hooked a thumb over his shoulder. 'This all started because the Diggers took a fancy to your oxen. All right. We'll give 'em two oxen, the mules, my spare horse. A peace offering, if you like, to guarantee us safe passage out of here. They might just be satisfied with that.'

'But what if they're not?' asked Conway. 'What if they still come after us?'

Eddings agreed. 'At least here we're forted up. On the move, they could shoot us down like dogs.'

'I'll be throwing a little something of

my own in to slow them down,' O'Brien replied grimly. 'Five bottles of liquid morphine. At a pinch they might mistake it for whiskey.' Ruefully he added, '*I* did.'

But Conway was still thinking about all the *ifs*. 'And if it doesn't? Dammit, O'Brien, see this from our side. We've got our families to think about, here. We can't just throw caution to the wind.'

Flat-eyed, O'Brien said quietly, 'If all that doesn't stop them from coming after you . . . there's always *me*.'

They stared across the low fire at him, horrified. Rose mouthed the word, *What?* O'Brien said, more businesslike now, 'There's a jumble of rocks about sixty, seventy yards back there a ways. I'll fort up there after you've gone, make sure the Diggers take what we leave 'em and then go. If it looks like they plan to follow you . . . well, I'll dissuade 'em.'

'But that's madness!' objected Kate. 'We can't allow you to do it! You'll be outnumbered and — '

'You people're talking like you've got a *choice* in the matter,' O'Brien broke in roughly. 'You haven't. You can't just sit tight and hope the Diggers'll go away. They won't. Not while they think there's easy pickings to be had here. Sooner or later you'll *have* to go. The supplies I packed in with me won't last forever, and you've already told me you're running low on ammunition.'

He looked at one fire-lit, frightened, sober face after another. 'You're damned if you do, and damned if you don't,' he murmured. 'And that's the sorry truth of it. But at least you stand a chance if you do like I say.'

The greenhorns exchanged looks, each unwilling to be the one to make the inevitable decision. O'Brien knelt and helped himself to coffee from a pot next to the fire while they held a desperate, whispered conference between themselves. At length Conway cleared his throat and said, 'All . . . all right, O'Brien. We'll go . . . if you think we really *can* make it. But . . . well, we truly *are* damned if we'll leave you behind. That's a thing we *won't* do.'

O'Brien regarded him over the rim of his cup. 'It won't be for long,' he replied, relieved that he'd won them over. 'I'll catch you up soon as I can.' He glanced north, into the darkness. 'You remember how the pass feeds out into a string of broad plains, about three or four miles further on?'

Conway nodded. 'Uh-huh. We saw them on our way in from the southeast.'

'Well, as you leave the pass, you'll see a stand of timber directly ahead of you, on the other side of the first slope, about five, six miles north. You head straight for that timber, and when you reach it, wait for me. If I don't come for you by noon — '

Rose said tremulously, 'Oh, Mr. O'Brien — '

He continued regardless. 'If I don't come for you by noon, you'll find a river on the far side of the trees. I think it's the Feather. You follow that west, and it should eventually lead you through the lower passes into Oroville. You got that? So long as you follow the river — '

Ashen-faced, Conway nodded more to shut him up than anything else. Clearly he didn't want to think about the sacrifice O'Brien might make by staying behind to deal with the Diggers. 'We . . . we understand.'

Eddings, throwing himself into it now that the decision had been made, said, 'We'll have to pack everything we need into one wagon. With what we've already butchered and what we're leaving for the Indians, we won't have enough oxen to haul them both.'

O'Brien nodded. 'That's right, so take only what you need and pack whatever's left into the spare wagon. You can always come back up here next spring to salvage what you can.' He hesitated a moment, then added, 'Your wife's body as well, if you like, Eddings.'

The widower froze. Secretly he'd been dreading having to leave her here alone.

'The cold'll preserve her till you're ready to take her home for a proper burial,' O'Brien told him softly.

Suddenly gratitude thawed Eddings' face and liquid moved in his deep eyes. He husked, 'Y-yes . . . it . . . it will, won't it?'

'Right,' O'Brien snapped. 'There's a lot to do and not much time to do it in, so let's get to work.'

Rose said, 'Do . . . do you *really* think we can do it, Mr. O'Brien?'

He looked at her, into her bloodshot eyes, trying to transfer some of his stubborn will to survive against all the odds into her with the force of his pale blue gaze alone. 'Ma'am,' he said, 'you've got four kids of your own and five nieces and nephews *relying* on you to do it. I'd say they were the nine best reasons in the world, wouldn't you? Now come on, let's get to work — you people're pulling out at dawn!'

7

They worked hard. Damned hard.

While O'Brien stood watch, they set about transferring their possessions from one wagon to the other, keeping only what they deemed vital aboard the Conestoga in which they planned to get away. They cleared out furniture and keepsakes and loaded up again with bedding and supplies, all the while trying to work around the sleeping children, and they worked with a relentless kind of frenzy, as if they wanted to keep too busy to pause and think, to weigh the risks and maybe lose their nerve.

They accomplished what they needed to do by midnight. Then O'Brien told them to get some rest.

Conway shook his head dismissively. 'You think we could sleep at a time like this?'

'Well, you'd better. You're going to need all your wits about you tomorrow.'

Breathing hard, Conway sleeved sweat off his face. 'Look, we've made up our minds. We're all packed up and ready to go. Why don't we just go now, instead of waiting till dawn?'

O'Brien put iron into his voice. 'Because if things don't go according to plan, this might be the last chance you get to rest up for a while. Maybe a *long* while.'

'That goes for you too,' said Eddings. 'Here, I've already slept. I'll stand watch now while *you* get some rest as well.'

O'Brien nodded readily. 'Thanks, Eddings. I'll relieve you at three.'

The greenhorns watched him settle into his corner, pull his blanket up and tilt his hat down over his face. Without purpose now, with nothing left to do but kill time, Conway and the women reluctantly followed his example, although they were too apprehensive to sleep.

Had they but known it, so was

O'Brien. Though he lay quiet and still, sleep eluded him just as it did the others. The responsibility of these men, women and children was heavy on him, and precluded sleep. He wanted to do his best by them, but couldn't help wondering if his best would be equal to the task.

Tiredly he listened to the rise and fall of the cold wind, the restless stirrings of the greenhorns, the sound of Eddings blowing into his hands, the shuffling of the animals, the creak and snap of wagon and canvas. Eventually he fell into a doze.

A couple of hours later he awoke with a jerk, pushed back his hat, dry-washed his face and climbed to his feet. Drawing his Winchester, he yawned. The cold had made him sluggish. As he weaved through all the sleeping figures huddled around the fire, he hoped it was having the same effect on the Diggers.

Eddings was sitting cross-legged beside one of the wagons, staring off into the darkness with a repeater across his lap. He jumped when O'Brien put a hand on his shoulder, and half twisted around.

'What — !'

'Shim.'

Eddings sagged with relief as O'Brien crouched beside him. O'Brien nodded towards the surrounding darkness. The landscape beyond was etched in gray and silver. 'All quiet out there?' he asked.

Eddings inclined his head. 'Uh-huh. It usually is, after dark. Arthur heard somewhere that Indians don't fight at night. That's why this bunch only bothers us during the day, I suppose. He says the only reason they chanced trying to steal the oxen at night last week was because they weren't expecting a fight.'

O'Brien scoured the shadows. 'He could be right,' he allowed. 'Some Indians *are* leery of fighting after dark. The Sioux, Cheyenne, Crow, Arapaho. But to others, the darkness is a weapon

— and some Indians'll use any weapon they can on you.'

'You sound like you're talking from experience.'

O'Brien took out the makings and rolled a cigarette. 'I am. Smoke?'

'No thanks.'

'Well, go grab an hour's sleep, if you can. I'll take over here now.'

Eddings grunted to his feet. 'I'm beyond sleep,' he said. 'But I think I'll go spend a little time . . . you know . . . with Alice. Before we leave.' He gave O'Brien an apologetic little smile and said quickly, 'I just can't get her out of my mind.'

O'Brien said, 'I'd be surprised if you could.'

'It's just that . . . me and Alice, we were . . . well, we got along well. *Real* well. Even if we get out of this alive . . . it's never going to be the same. Not for me.'

'Time heals, Eddings. You might not think so now, but it *does*, believe me.'

Eddings cocked an eyebrow at him.

'Is that experience talking again?' he asked.

O'Brien nodded, and for a moment then his thoughts turned to another time and place, and a girl calling his name the moment before she died.

When Eddings was gone, O'Brien studied the quiet, windswept pass. After a time, Eddings crept back into camp and lay down. An hour passed. At last O'Brien got up, crossed over to the animals and set to work. One by one, he dragged the two oxen, both mules and the zebra dun over to a spot thirty yards away, past all the formless mounds that marked the positions of the dead Diggers, and tethered them around a scanty show of brush. The oxen went without argument, calm, unhurried, resigned to whatever a largely uncharitable Fate had in store for them. He had more of a problem with the ornery mules. And when he came to the ageing dun, his thoughts turned once more to Charlie.

Finally he took out the five brown-glass bottles he'd found in Charlie's gear and spilled a little of the cherry brandy McGovern had given them around the neck and stopper of each one in turn, to disguise the off-putting smell of morphine. Then he carried them over to the tethered animals and stood them up in the snow a few feet away, where they couldn't fail to be seen.

In the low light it looked a paltry offering. But there was no telling how the Diggers' primitive minds would work. To them this might be a king's ransom. To them it might be *enough*.

Well, a body could hope.

As he followed the well-worn path back through the snow, he saw that the greenhorns were up and doing, the women waking reluctant children, the men lowering the wagon tongue with its red shirt pennant so that they could hitch up the remaining oxen.

Rose asked O'Brien if they had time to heat some coffee. He told her yes, because they wouldn't be stopping for anything more substantial, not any time soon.

They drank the coffee while it was still scalding. Then he saddled his mustang, wiped his weapons over, methodically checked and dried all his cartridges. Conway and Eddings finished hitching the team. The older children helped load the younger ones into the back of the wagon. They kicked snow over the fire, put the remainder of their gear away, and climbed into saddle, or wagon, or wagon-box.

At last they were ready to go.

O'Brien said quietly, 'Let's do it.'

Eddings, standing beside the team, slapped the oxen with a quirt, and as the big slab-shouldered beasts put their weight into it, the massive Conestoga lumbered forward, snow churning up beneath its heavy wheels, canvas awning quivering with every rut and pothole they passed over.

The animals they'd left behind them watched them go.

The pre-dawn was lonely, raw and indistinct. O'Brien angled his horse alongside the wagon, Winchester balanced across his lap. They trundled on for seventy yards, then came to a halt. O'Brien turned the horse around, stood up in the stirrups and put out his hand.

'Well, Conway,' he said, 'from here on out, you're on your own. Good luck.'

Up on the high wagon seat, Conway took his hand and squeezed it. 'We'll be waiting for you in that timber,' he replied.

O'Brien looked at the two women, who were just visible in the puckered oxbow behind him, then across to Eddings, and nodded. 'Now get out of here,' he said.

He watched the wagon rumble ponderously away, then dismounted and led the mustang up into the confusion of rocks he'd spotted the day before. With his mount securely tied, he found himself a well-protected spot from which he could keep an eye on the animals they'd left for the Diggers. All he could do after that was wait — and maybe offer up a prayer that this would work.

Thirty minutes passed. Glassy-eyed, O'Brien kept his attention focused on their back-trail. Slowly the sky grew imperceptibly lighter, and he found himself wondering how far the green-horns had managed to get.

Then, without any warning whatsoever, he saw the first of the Diggers break away from the shadows a few yards beyond the tethered animals, and work their way slowly forward.

Instinctively he tightened his grip on the Winchester.

He counted three of them; no, four . . . five . . . half a dozen, just blobs of liquid shadow at first, until they gradually resolved into the silhouettes of men, crouching and slinking steadily nearer, moving more like apes than men.

He saw Charlie's dun tug at his tie-rope as the Diggers came closer.

Four of the Indians encircled the animals and inspected them in the building light. The other two kept coming, clutching rifles to their chests. They closed on the abandoned wagon with much caution, surveyed it from every angle, then finally peered inside.

Seeing them clearer now, seeing their dark, grimy faces set within the framework of their long unkempt black hair, seeing their heavy brows and graceless lumberings as they pulled furniture from the wagon and cast it carelessly aside, seeing the macabre mixture of white-man hand-me-downs they wore and the number of weapons each man carried about him — knives, hatchets, clubs, handguns, long guns, lances, even a couple of curved sabers — O'Brien recalled the five Diggers he'd killed twenty-four hours earlier, and shuddered.

The half-dozen Indians out there now were suddenly joined by nine more. They came out from behind the rocks and brush further along Klamath

Pass, and divided their attention between the animals and the deserted campsite. Like the greenhorns, they wore blankets, blanket jackets, coats, ponchos, anything to keep themselves warm.

Their voices carried to him, though he could understand nothing of their guttural growlings. The meaning was plain enough, however. They were asking themselves where the greenhorns had gone and why, and why they'd left these apparently sound animals behind them. Judging by all the gesturing that was going on, a few of them at least were suggesting that they should go after the fleeing whites, finish them off and then help themselves to everything they'd taken with them.

O'Brien was afraid it might go that way.

But it was by no means cut and dried. There was more debate. Indians liked nothing better than speechifying, and these Diggers were no different.

So it went on, arguments for and

arguments against. More Indians arrived, eight more, most of them mounted on ribby ponies, the rest on despondent, ill-treated mules. They were leading a cavvy of other, similar mounts with them, the mounts of the men who had come on ahead of them, afoot.

O'Brien did a swift head-count of the Indians and muttered, 'Twenty-three . . . '

The arrival of these newcomers led to some more heated discussion. One man alone seemed to do more talking than any of the others. He was tall and lithe, with two bedraggled eagle feathers tucked into the band of his old Hardee hat and a scar in the shape of a lightning fork coursing down the left side of his cruel, unwashed face.

O'Brien had a sneaking suspicion that he might be their leader, or as much of a leader as such a tribe of degenerates would be likely to acknowledge.

It looked as if the man was trying to

convince his brothers to go after the greenhorns. And worse still, it didn't appear as if the rest of them needed much persuading any more.

Five minutes later they reached their decision, and the Diggers who had come ahead on foot started towards their mounts.

O'Brien whispered, 'Aw, shoot . . . '

But then one of them spotted the bottles of morphine standing up in the snow a few feet from the oxen.

Things would start to get interesting now.

The rest of the Indians gathered round. One of them snatched up a bottle and another one tried to grab it away from him. There was a brief struggle. The first Digger dropped the bottle. It hit a rock and shattered.

Tempers frayed at once, and suddenly the fight assumed a new and more deadly intensity. The second man produced a knife. So did the first. They circled each other warily, suddenly charged in, struggled some more, fell apart, met again and —

The second man hunched up. O'Brien heard the moan that fell from between his slack lips. He backed away from his opponent, slid off the man's bloody knife, clutched his streaming stomach and keeled over.

There followed a brief silence; then, as one, the rest of the Diggers descended upon the four remaining bottles, booting the freshly dead Indian out of their path.

Later they would strip him of every possession he owned.

The bottles were passed from one eager mouth to the next. He watched as morphine splashed from bottle-necks and spilled over bronze chins, and listened to the Indians' subsequent roars of laughter. He wondered how much of an effect the contents of four bottles would have on twenty-two men and decided grimly that it wouldn't have even half the effect he'd been hoping for.

One by one the bottles were drained

and hurled disgustedly against rocks. A few of the Diggers started stumbling as though drunk. Maybe they were, or maybe they just *thought* they were. Several more bent over or fell to their knees and were sick. But the majority still looked stone-cold sober and in complete control of their faculties.

O'Brien shook his head slowly. But at least the sudden binge had distracted the Indians from their original course. How long that would last, how much extra time it would buy the greenhorns, was anyone's guess.

He watched the Diggers mill around without purpose, and told himself that even a modest jolt of the opiate must work *some* kind of disorientating effect upon them.

The fellow with the eagle feathers in his hat claimed Charlie's dun for his own, and took out a knife, strode over to the tucked-up, weaving claybank he'd ridden in on and unceremoniously slit its throat.

The horse collapsed with its legs

folded under it. The watching Diggers seemed to find that funny. O'Brien glanced away with a grimace. Like all men of the range worth their salt, he hated to see cruelty or suffering inflicted upon any animal. To kill a horse was one thing. In the case of the claybank, it was probably a blessing. But to kill a horse, to kill *anything*, so casually . . .

Two of Eagle Feathers' friends helped themselves to the mules, and promptly slit the throats of their own wind-broken mounts before transferring their hide saddles to their new acquisitions. A few of the watching Indians then came forward to butcher the carcasses, and after that they fixed a fire and dined on rough-cooked claybank steaks.

About an hour later, Eagle Feathers suddenly sprang to his feet and started making another speech. He pointed to the oxen, to the abandoned wagon, to the direction in which the greenhorns had gone. He talked up a real storm, not that O'Brien understood a word of it, but once again, his meaning was clear enough.

The more he talked, the more O'Brien felt his innards tightening. There was nothing left between the greenhorns and the Diggers now except him. But even now it might not come to a confrontation. All it needed was for a couple of Diggers to shake their heads and say no, and they might simply mount up and herd the oxen back to wherever they'd made their camp, and spend the rest of the day impressing their women with tall tales of how they'd scared the crazy white-eyes away.

He watched Eagle Feathers chatter on, studied the reactions of the listening Indians. He didn't much like what he saw.

Some minutes later they leapt up, brandishing their many weapons, and with much posturing and chest-puffing, they headed for their horses and mules.

They were going after the greenhorns.

Again O'Brien muttered, 'Aw, shoot . . . '

He looked around. He had his Winchester with him, his Colt fully loaded, the war bag containing the rest of his ammunition within reach. The Diggers had superior numbers, but he had the advantage of height, cover and surprise. He was better organized, better armed —

He thought, *Face it, O'Brien — you're going to die out here.*

A few of the Diggers stripped the canvas off the wagon and quickly rooted through its contents. They took everything they were likely to want, and set fire to the rest.

O'Brien's lip curled and the voice inside his head said coolly, *You destructive sonsofbitches . . .*

Mounted now, the Diggers started down the pass towards him at a jog, with Eagle Feathers in the lead and the rest, fairly thirsting for combat now, crowding in close behind. Thick black smoke began to funnel up into the frosty air as the fire took hold of the wagon. Again O'Brien shook his head, appalled as he always was by the senselessness of such behavior.

He brought the Winchester up to his shoulder, running everything that was now about to happen through his mind, forcing himself to settle down, grow dead calm, killing calm, rehearsing it all so that there would be no mistakes when hell finally broke loose.

The Diggers closed the gap between them by half. O'Brien drew a bead on Eagle Feathers' chest and took up first pressure on the trigger. He knew that this would be a battle he couldn't hope to win. No matter what he might tell himself to the contrary, the odds were simply too great. The best he could do was inflict as much damage on the Diggers as he could, to slow them down and convince them the hard way that any further pursuit of the greenhorns just wasn't worth it.

The Indians drew nearer, their mounts slushing through the crusty snow. O'Brien's finger tightened still further on the trigger —

Suddenly a shout rang out from somewhere back down the pass, and the advancing Diggers hauled in and hipped around. Aware of the tension that made the Diggers stiffen abruptly, O'Brien raised his line of vision from the barrel of the Winchester and focused on the murky pass behind them.

He didn't see anyone right away. Neither did the Diggers. But a wave of ominous muttering washed through them as they turned their assortment of mounts around to face the wall of smoke billowing sideways now from the blazing wagon, effectively turning their backs on him.

At last a movement caught his eye. Twelve riders came through the drifting smoke in a slow-moving strung-out line.

Twelve more Diggers.

O'Brien sagged, heart sinking, and swore under his breath. Christ, if the odds had been lousy before, they were positively *suicidal now.*

Eagle Feathers watched them come. In all respects the newcomers were mirror images of his own men, save for a grossly fat Indian in a thick woolen overcoat that still bore the blood of its previous owner as a stain over the heart. His appearance sent another buzz through the watching Diggers. Obviously he was someone important to them, someone to be feared, but O'Brien didn't know enough about their culture to hazard a guess who he might be. He wasn't even certain that they *had* a culture.

A moment passed, and then Eagle Feathers kicked the dun into movement and walked the animal back through his men to meet the new arrivals. The fat Digger reined in and followed his approach through glittering eyes.

As soon as he was near enough, the fat Digger lashed out with a speed that belied his size and smashed Eagle Feathers in the side of the head. Eagle

Feathers swayed and almost fell out of the saddle, but managed to hold on. He shook his head to clear it, spat a stream of blood into the snow and then barked what was no doubt the Digger equivalent of, 'What the hell was *that* for?'

The fat man snapped his angry reply. He had a smooth, womanish face, and his jowls were so fleshy that they pushed his eyes up into piggy little slits. Lines of red and yellow paint adorned his face, and shaggy black hair frayed out from under a woman's poke bonnet. All in all, he was just about the strangest man O'Brien had ever seen.

He prattled on at Eagle Feathers, using one grimy forefinger to indicate the burning wagon, the slaughtered animals and the still-tethered oxen while he spoke. O'Brien got the impression that the fat Digger had been drawn to Klamath Pass by the column of smoke, that he was mad at Eagle Feathers for burning a perfectly good wagon, and for leaving the partly butchered carcasses and the oxen behind while he and his brothers went off in pursuit of a bunch of whites who had already cost them dearly enough as it was. When he pointed to all the shattered glass and hit Eagle Feathers again, it became pretty obvious that he was kind of annoyed at having missed out on what had passed for booze as well.

Eagle Feathers' band of Diggers were walking their horses and mules closer to the two now, the better to watch and listen to what was quickly shaping up to be something of a showdown.

O'Brien sank down behind the rocks and quickly considered the new position. To stay here and try to hold back better than forty Indians was going to be impossible. But perhaps he might not have to, if the fat Digger decreed that they should cut their losses and let the crazy whites go free.

He tried to calculate the time. The greenhorns had had, what, about two hours' head start on the Indians. If they hadn't already reached the timber, they couldn't be far off.

He risked another look over the rocks. Eagle Feathers and the fat Digger were still arguing, the rest of their men still watching them.

It came to him then that he was never going to get a better chance than this to light out.

Reaching his decision, he pulled cautiously back from the rocks, then turned and started down towards his horse.

Thirty feet away, a Digger Indian was standing beside the animal, watching him.

O'Brien froze.

For the next quarter of a minute they just stood watching each other. The Digger was short, bow-legged and broad through the chest. It was hard to put an age to him, but he was certainly no more than thirty. He wore a threadbare plaid jacket over an old cavalry shirt and fringed buckskin leggings tucked into old cavalry-issue boots. He had an arrow nocked in the string of a long, curved bow, an ancient Colt Paterson in a holster on his left hip and a long, rusty-bladed skinning knife jammed into his belt on the right.

O'Brien looked at his scarred, disease-ravaged face and wondered briefly where he'd come from. But that wasn't important right now. What mattered was the bow and arrow in his fists, the fact that he might not be here alone.

All at once the momentary lull ended and the Digger brought his bow up, drew back the string and loosed the arrow at him. O'Brien threw himself to the side as the shaft drilled through the thin air and clattered against the rocks.

Having missed him, the Digger threw down the bow and snatched at his Colt. Knowing he couldn't afford the sound of a gunshot, not if he wanted to get out of here undetected, O'Brien threw his Winchester at him, then came after it at a run. He smashed into the buck at waist level and took the two of them crashing into the rocks to their right.

They hit the ground in a tangle and rolled. Rocks jabbed each man through his thick winter clothing. The Indian tried to twist O'Brien's face out of shape. O'Brien squeezed his eyes tight shut as his opponent made a move to gouge them out.

Then he got the Indian onto his back, sat on him, and started slamming him against the rocks to knock him out. The Indian struggled to unseat him. He was a strong sonuver as well, and suddenly O'Brien was flung sideways, off him.

As the Digger sprang up and tried to stomp him, O'Brien rolled away from him, grabbed a handful of snow and flung it at him. The oncoming Indian grunted, slewed to a halt, tried to paw the snow out of his eyes. O'Brien came up, hit him in the belly, brushed his hands away from his face, hit him on the jaw. The Digger lost his balance and fell. O'Brien followed him down. They struggled some more, squirming through the snow, the Digger wriggling like an eel on a chopping block. His right hand snaked down towards the knife on his hip. Seeing that, O'Brien did the only thing he could — he grabbed up a fist-sized rock close by, brought it back, then down on the Digger's head.

It made a very wet cracking sound.

The Digger went still and the light went out of his dark, spiteful eyes. O'Brien sagged over him, gasping for air, and let the rock tumble from his loose fingers. A moment later he shoved away from the Indian and clambered to his feet. He didn't think they'd made enough noise during the struggle to alert the rest of the Diggers, but he figured he'd better take a look just to make sure, and then get the hell out of there.

Bending to retrieve the Winchester, he started back towards the rocks.

That was when he heard a soft whisper of sound behind him.

Spinning around, he saw the Digger he thought he'd killed struggling back up, his face a mask of blood in which only eye-whites and teeth showed clearly.

The Digger had drawn and leveled his Colt.

O'Brien dropped down and to one side, swearing as the .36 blasted through the air and powdered rock close to where he'd just been.

With the alarm now well and truly sounded, he braced the Winchester against his hip and returned fire. The bullet smacked into the Indian's stout torso and threw him back into the snow with a watery gurgle. Even as his heels finished kicking ruts into the snow, O'Brien was heading for the mustang at a run. He heard raised voices coming back down the pass, slammed his rifle into the scabbard, quickly tied his war bag around the saddle horn and then hauled himself up across leather. He knew it wasn't likely to be much of a chase. His horse had the beating of all the animals he'd seen among the Diggers, including Charlie's old dun.

But the sooner he got out of there, the better he'd like it.

As he heeled the mustang in the sides and the horse lumbered forward through the snow, O'Brien threw a look over his shoulder. The Diggers were already starting after him, whatever enmity that existed between Eagle Feathers and the fat man now temporarily set aside. Gunshots peppered the air, and O'Brien leaned lower in the saddle to make himself a smaller target. His mustang slipped on the uncertain footing, regained balance and kept going.

He sent the animal cannoning through the ravine with the Diggers giving chase the best way they knew how, and gradually the gap between them widened, as he had known it would.

But what if there were any more of the bastards up ahead? What if he was fleeing one bunch of savages only to run slap-bang into another?

Aw shoot . . .

8

Somehow he made it through the pass in one piece, and sent the horse streaking on across the vast, snowy tract beyond at a reckless gallop.

The wheel-ruts the Conestoga had left to mark its passage curved across the ice-encrusted snow like two blue-gray scars that gradually met before disappearing into the faraway timber. O'Brien sent the mustang after them, but already it had been a long, arduous run and the animal was breathing hard and starting to stumble.

Midway across the great plain he had no choice but to rein down and give the horse a breather. He was gasping himself as he dismounted, sending out great clouds of mist to fog the bleak forenoon.

Turning around, he looked back the way he'd come. He saw nothing and frankly didn't expect to. Still, he reached into his saddlebag, brought out his field glasses and trained them on the mouth of the pass. They only confirmed what he'd already figured.

He deflated a little, leaned against the horse and put his forehead on his sleeve. To be honest, he didn't know if the Diggers would bother to pursue him all the way to the timber or not. He felt that there was a pretty good chance that they wouldn't, but with Indians you could never be sure. One thing *was* certain, though. If they *did* come after him, it would be out of greed, not any desire to avenge their fallen comrades. The Diggers were indifferent to death, so callous that they had no real grasp of bereavement and no true need for revenge.

No; you could put everything they'd done to date down to greed, plain and simple. And whatever they chose to do now would be no different.

Absurdly, he was sweating. Drawing in a deep breath, he palmed his wet face and remounted. He tried to push the mustang back up to a run but the horse protested and started sidestepping. If he'd had the option, he'd have let the animal choose its own pace, but the plain fact was that he *didn't* have the option. For a few moments they fought a contest of wills. When O'Brien won, the mustang fell into a steady lope.

The trees grew nearer and he tried to convince himself that they'd seen the last of the Diggers. It wasn't worth their while to chase him all this way, especially that fat buck in the woman's bonnet. He didn't look as if he moved around anymore than he could help.

He reached the timber about forty minutes later and found the greenhorns roughly halfway in, hunkering beside a small fire a few yards from the wagon. As he rode in they got to their feet and came to surround him, relief showing on the faces of the adults, the expressions of the children revealing only fear and uncertainty.

They all started asking questions at

once, but O'Brien quietened them with a raised palm. 'Everyone aboard the wagon,' he snapped tautly. 'We're getting out of here.'

Conway raised scared hazel eyes to him and asked anxiously, 'The redguts?'

'I don't know if they're coming or not,' O'Brien replied honestly. 'I don't think they will, but . . . '

Conway nodded and booted snow over the fire. Rose, Kate and Eddings quickly loaded the children into the back of the wagon. Conway climbed up to the wagon seat and Eddings boosted both the women into the back with the children. Finally the widower hustled up front and whacked the oxen with his quirt and then they were moving again.

O'Brien forged out ahead, the blood coursing through him still. He cantered through the dim, largely silent timber, heading for the faintly rippling water just visible on the other side of the bosque. Ten minutes later the trees gave way to a strip of undulating, boulder-littered land that ran alongside the bulrush-fringed bank of the Feather River.

Quickly he scoured the area. At this point the river stretched two hundred feet from one thickly wooded, shaggy bank to the other. Although he spotted several animal tracks in the snow leading down to the muddy brown water, there was nothing to indicate that any two-legged moccasin- or boot-wearing creatures had been this way recently.

He turned the horse and rode back to the slow-moving rattling wagon, dismayed by the meager progress the greenhorns had made.

Reining down, he said, 'Can't you go any faster?'

Conway shook his head. 'You can't rush oxen. They go at their own pace or they don't go at all.'

'Well, do your best with 'em. When you reach the river, turn 'em west and keep going.'

Conway nodded. 'What about you?'

'I want to take another look at our back trail.'

He turned the mustang around the wagon and blurred back through the trees. When he reached the timber's edge he reined in, took out his field glasses, raised himself up in his stirrups and scanned the broken country to the south and west. Almost immediately his eyes snagged on something midway across the snowfield.

'Dammit!'

Black steadily moving dots against the stark white backdrop, the Indians were easy to spot, and there was certainly no mistaking the two riders out front of the main bunch — Eagle Feathers and the fat Digger.

He twisted the horse around and loped back to the wagon. It hardly seemed to have moved at all. As he brought his mount to a halt, Eddings turned to face him and the women appeared in the canvas horseshoe at the back of the wagon, all of them sensing from his manner that he had bad news to impart.

He said, 'You'd better get your oxen to start picking their feet up, Conway.'

Conway squinted at him. The Indians?'

He nodded.

'How many?'

'About forty.'

Suddenly Kate spoke out. 'How much time do we have?'

O'Brien glanced at her. 'Fifteen, twenty minutes. Maybe a little longer.'

Conway nodded brusquely and slapped the reins across the team's broad, slabby backs. 'Giddup, there!'

The wagon labored on, its progress tortuous and inchmeal. O'Brien watched it go, then rode back to the edge of the timber. It seemed to him that the Indians had made better progress across the snowfield than anyone aboard a half-starved horse or mule had any right to expect.

He rejoined the wagon. It was only yards from the riverbank now. A couple of the younger children, sensing the tension of the moment, had started crying. Conway looked down at him from the high seat, his face flushed and sweat-run, his dark eyes pools of despair. He took one look at O'Brien's expression and said with scary calm, 'We're not going to make it, are we? I mean, even if we start following the river, it's only a matter of time before they catch up with us, isn't it?'

Eddings flung down his quirt. 'Dammit, O'Brien!' he flared. 'We put our trust in you!'

O'Brien pinned them both with a hard look, his jaw muscles flexing beneath his beard. The greenhorns were watching him, waiting for him to tell them that it was all going to be fine. But it *wasn't* going to be fine. The situation was slipping away from him. Rapidly. And he had to think of something to stop that from happening. But what?

He said, 'I told you I'd get you out of here, and that's what I aim to do.'

His mind was racing so fast now that he feared he might lose control of it altogether. But something was beginning to come together at last, something insane but just possible, something dangerous but no more dangerous than sitting here waiting for the Diggers to arrive.

Gesturing to a small box fixed to the left side of the wagon, he said, 'You got a hatchet in that toolbox there, Eddings?'

Eddings nodded.

'Well, get it and head for those saplings yonder. I want two of 'em cut down to about eight or nine feet apiece. Trim 'em as best you can, then stow 'em in back of the wagon until we need 'em.'

'Huh?'

Ignoring him, O'Brien centered his attention on Conway. 'When you get to the riverbank, turn the wagon around and wedge rocks behind the wheels to make sure it doesn't go rolling back. Then unlimber the oxen, raise the wagon-tongue and lash it to the box.'

Bewildered, Conway said, 'What in God's name — '

O'Brien said, 'We're turning your wagon into a boat, Conway. And when we've done that, we're riding the river *out* of here.'

Conway shook his head as the others gasped and muttered. 'You're out of your senses! This wagon'll never stay afloat! It's too heavy.'

'It'd be better if we could take the wheels off, I grant you, but we don't have the time for that,' O'Brien replied. 'It'll float, though, don't fret. They don't call 'em prairie schooners for nothing.'

'You're going to get us all killed!' breathed Eddings.

'Just *do* it!' O'Brien barked, turning the horse around.

Conway said, 'And you?'

O'Brien drew his Winchester. 'I'll try to buy you some extra time.'

'Against forty savages?'

'Got any better ideas?'

Eddings piped up. 'Uh-huh. Let me get my rifle and I'll come back with you.'

'No, Jimmy.'

All eyes turned as Kate Eddings clambered awkwardly from the back of the wagon and trotted over to O'Brien, her brother's Henry repeater in her small hands. 'You've already got a job to do. *I'll* help Mr. O'Brien.'

O'Brien said, 'You can put that notion right out of your mind, ma'am. It's like I said last night — what I've got planned's not my idea of woman's work.'

She looked up at him with defiance plain on her pale, oval face. 'And as I told *you*, Mr. O'Brien, you might be sur — '

There wasn't time to argue about it. O'Brien threw a look at the men. 'You know what to do,' he said. 'Fire three shots into the air when everything's set.'

Then he turned the horse and galloped away, Kate yelling his name after him as he went.

By the time he achieved the timber's edge again, the Diggers were no more than three hundred yards away. He came out of the saddle even before the mustang skidded to a halt, quickly tied the animal back among the trees, unhooked his war bag and hurried the rest of the way forward in a crouch.

He went down behind some dead wood and watched the Diggers ride ever closer. They were bunched together behind their two leaders — very sloppy — and following the wagon tracks in jocular mood, like they really couldn't wait for the killing to start.

Gently O'Brien pumped a .44/40 into the breech, thinking, *Just you hang in there, fellers. The killing'll start soon enough.*

He tried to clear his mind of everything but the job at hand, but couldn't shake the idea that he'd failed the people he'd come to help. Maybe Conway was right. Maybe he *had* lost his senses. And maybe Eddings was right as well; maybe he *was* going to get them all killed. But what the hell choice did he have?

He felt his temper slipping and quickly moved to dampen it down. A man in this business couldn't afford a temper. You had to be as cold and dispassionate as you could, though it was rarely as easy as that.

With renewed determination he shunted everything else to the back of his mind. The Indians came on, shortening the distance from two hundred yards to one hundred, from one hundred to fifty . . .

O'Brien thought irritably, *Come on, you bastards, let's get it over and done with.*

When they were a little under forty yards away he pulled in a breath, came up over the dead wood and started shooting.

He took them completely by surprise, as he'd known he would. He worked the Winchester's action, fired, worked it and fired again, and every bullet he sent buzzing among them helped throw them into disarray.

Teeth clenched, ears protesting at the gun-thunder, he emptied the long gun into them. He went for Eagle Feathers first, blasted him twice in the chest so that he careened back off Charlie's dun like a sack of wet wheat and didn't move again once he hit the ground. Then he switched aim, lined up on the fat Digger who'd been riding beside him, quickly sent him to the Happy Hunting Ground with one bullet in the face and another in his blubbery belly.

He took no pleasure in what he was doing, he wasn't proud of it, but he'd known from the start that there could be no reasoning with such savages, so it just had to be done this way instead; and out ahead of him the bunched Indians broke and scattered, and some made it to cover while the rest screamed and raised their hands and tumbled sideways off their mounts to roll or writhe in pain.

Still he kept the Winchester working,

empty shell cases hurling up out of the ejector at the top of the weapon to spin dully in the watery midday sunshine before tinkling to earth around him. Then the gun was empty, and he ducked back out of sight as, finally, his opponents recovered from their shock and started shooting back.

He grabbed the war bag, spilled out fresh cartridges and set about reloading. For a long few seconds a savage fusillade chopped through the surrounding woods. Then, abruptly, it fell silent. O'Brien froze, listening but not really surprised. The Diggers probably didn't have so much ammunition that they could afford to waste any. They'd want something to shoot *at* before they used up any more.

He peered through brittle foliage to see how much damage he'd done. It wasn't as bad as it had first seemed. The snow was littered with three dead men and another on the verge, mottled with spilled blood and discarded weapons. Two wounded braves were begging their brothers for help. Riderless horses and mules were standing around them with rawhide reins dangling.

He finished reloading the rifle and tried to prepare himself for the reprisal he knew must come sooner or later. Somewhere back in the forest a twig snapped and he threw a quick look behind him just as Kate Eddings came blundering towards him through the underbrush.

'Aw, for — !'

One of the Indians spotted her. A gun blast cracked through the air and another volley quickly followed it. O'Brien made a sharp movement with his flattened right hand and hissed, 'Get down!' She did, and snaked the rest of the way to join him, still clutching her brother's rifle.

He put his eyes back on the corpse-strewn snowfield, again not surprised by this new development but sure as hell angered by it. She also peered through the brush to scan the battle-site, and he heard her gasp when she saw the carnage he had wrought.

That made him look at her. Her face was flushed from the run she had made to get back here on foot. Her lips were clamped tight, her eyes taking on a kind of glaze as she looked upon a scene she had never previously thought to see. She was scared, but she was fighting it.

'Come to lend a hand?' he asked bitterly.

Stiffly she said, 'Yes. I mean it, Mr. O'Brien. You — '

Putting his eyes back on the scene ahead of them, he said, 'How're your folks making out?'

They think you're mad,' she told him bluntly. 'They think you're going to get them all killed. But they're doing what you told them, because they can't think of anything better.'

He smiled mirthlessly. 'And what do you think?'

Her eyes moved over his profile. 'If we're going to die,' she replied, calmly now, 'I can think of no better way to go than in defense of my brother's children.'

He stiffened suddenly, making her start. As he scanned the battlefield with bleak eyes, he temporarily set aside the admiration he felt for her and brought his Winchester back up.

'What is it?' she whispered.

He said quietly, 'They're coming again.'

She looked out across the snow and saw them. The remaining Indians had dismounted, spread out and were bellying slowly forward, using the drifts for cover.

O'Brien said, 'Best if you go back to the wagon now, Miss Kate.'

'No. I came to help — '

'Go back, I said!'

She shook her head stubbornly. 'I said I've come to help! You're only one man, Mr. O'Brien. You can't fight them *all* on your own!'

Frustration tied his tongue. 'Well . . . at least keep your head down till it's all over.'

He watched them inch closer. Inside his gloves his hands felt clammy. The Indians waited until they were within about twenty yards of his position and then one of them leapt up, screamed something vile and came charging forward, and within seconds Kate was screaming too, because the other Indians were following his lead, and it was a terrifying sight to behold.

O'Brien came up with flame lancing from the Winchester's round barrel and empty cases spewing into the air before his eyes. Diggers buckled up under the hail of lead, grabbed themselves, spun around and fell, or turned tail altogether.

Then it was over again, as quickly as that; the Diggers melted back into hiding, left a handful of dead or wounded behind them, and when O'Brien glanced sideways and saw smoke curling from the barrel of Kate's Henry repeater, he realized that she'd done what she'd said she'd do — fight alongside him.

She was trembling violently and tears were crawling down her cheeks, but she made no sound, voiced nothing of the horror she must be feeling inside.

Gentling his voice he said, 'All right, ma'am. You've done your bit here. Get on back to your folks now.' Her hazel eyes grazed his face as he went on, 'Take my horse. I'll pull back on foot, make sure they keep their distance.'

At last she opened her mouth to tell him that she was staying, but before she could speak, three gun blasts suddenly sounded from the other side of the forest, and they looked each other in the face.

Three gunshots.

Everything was set. The wagon was ready.

Again he said, 'Go *on*,' and this time he deliberately put so much urgency into the words that she felt compelled, albeit reluctantly, to obey them. Still in shock, she mouthed something that could have been *good luck*, or *hurry, then*, and edged carefully away from the dead wood before scurrying to his horse.

O'Brien stifled the impulse to watch her go, kept a look-out instead, and when the drum of hoof beats receded into the distance a few moments later, and one of the Diggers eighty feet away poked his head up to find out what was going on, O'Brien put a bullet into the air above him that told him to mind his own beeswax.

After that it fell as still and quiet as granite, and O'Brien felt his edginess growing more acute. Maybe the Diggers were gathering themselves for another full-frontal charge, or trying to worm around and come up on him from the flanks. Maybe even now —

He waited another full minute, then gathered his gear together and withdrew slowly and quietly, keeping his head down and hugging cover until he was sure that the thicker trees would screen him from the Diggers. Only then did he straighten up and fall into a lope.

It was only a matter of time before the Indians realized he was gone, of course. After that they would come forward in a swarm and the chase would be well and truly on. But maybe they would hang back long enough for him to build up a sizeable lead on them.

He'd only gone ninety or a hundred feet when a single gunshot sounded distantly behind him.

His jaws bunched up again. One of them was trying to draw his fire so that the rest could get a decent crack at him the minute he showed his face to shoot back. Trouble was, he was no longer there *to* shoot back. And once the Diggers realized that . . .

He jogged on at a steady, tireless pace, glancing back every few yards. Another gunshot spat into the trees behind him, and he got a sudden mental picture of the Diggers starting to wonder if he was still where they thought he was or not, of them slowly beginning to realize that maybe he wasn't — and then, a vivid image of them advancing tentatively on hands and knees to the little patch of dead wood from which he'd made his stand, finding it empty . . .

He thought he heard someone behind him shouting, but maybe that was only his imagination playing tricks on him again. There was another single gun blast, and as that died away he *did* hear shouting, and knew he'd been found out at last.

He broke into a flat-out run.

He heard them blundering deeper into the forest, howling their rage at his deceit. He looked back, saw ten, twenty of them racing through patches of pale daylight a hundred-fifty feet away, darting from tree to tree, jabbing accusing fingers at him.

He turned, brought the Winchester up to his cheek and sent three hasty shots back at them. As they dived for cover, he turned away and sprinted on, breathing hard now, feeling a stitch in his side.

More howling; a sudden rattle of gunfire. He broke into a crazy zigzag to confound his pursuers, put his head down, tried to concentrate only on running faster —

The ground sped along beneath him like a loamy brown treadmill. He leapt over a deadfall, landing badly on one ankle and staggered a few paces until the pain subsided and he could pick up speed again. Another crackling of gunfire; the slightly hollow *pock* of lead splintering tree-bark nearby. Doggedly he ran on, hastened by arrow and lance.

There was a lot of shouting now, too close for comfort, and for a moment he wondered if he'd been so intent on maintaining the pace that he hadn't noticed them gaining on him. But then something else entered his blinkered awareness, the sound of rushing water, and when he looked up he saw the wagon sitting on the riverbank ahead of him, the greenhorns crowding into the oxbow behind the seat, Conway slamming a rifle to his shoulder beside the wagon, all of them yelling themselves hoarse as they urged him on, and almost before he knew it he was bursting out of the trees, tossing his rifle and war bag up to Eddings.

'All . . . all . . . set?' he panted.

Eddings said gravely, 'This had better work.'

Conway fired a quick flurry of shots into his distant pursuers. The yells of the Diggers echoed flatly through the forest as they slowed, bellied down, came on more cautiously.

O'Brien told Conway to get into the wagon while he kicked the rocks out from behind its wheels. The greenhorn gave him no argument. Gunfire erupted from somewhere far back in the trees, and the children who weren't already crying started to scream. O'Brien staggered around the wagon, working feverishly against the clock until at last the final rock was kicked away and Conway put out a hand and dragged him up into the box.

O'Brien fell in, came up on hands

and knees, turned around.

Nothing was happening.

Rose husked, 'We're not m-moving!'

The wagon was crammed full of blankets, provisions and screeching children, and the noise of it all was tremendous. O'Brien snapped, 'Hand me one of those saplings!' and Eddings hurried to comply, fumbling in his haste.

O'Brien grasped the pole, shoved it out through the oxbow until the far end struck the ground at an angle, then pushed against it, pushed with teeth clenching and muscles straining.

Still nothing happened.

'Get the other pole!' O'Brien yelled. 'Quick!'

Conway took it from Eddings, did as O'Brien was doing, and behind them Eddings whispered, 'Come on, come on . . . ' and the women went, 'Shhh, shhh,' to the scared children —

Almost imperceptibly the wagon moved. They pushed harder, and slowly the wheels turned another few inches, slipping a little on all the detritus that littered the bank. Eddings raised his voice — 'Come on, come on, *COME ON*' — and they shoved still harder, harder, so hard it seemed that the saplings might splinter.

But then . . .

. . . all at once, the wagon started rolling, gathered momentum, trundled down the river bank, ass-end splashing into the cold water with a crash that sent up a massive explosion of white spray around it, and the women and children were screaming, Conway and Eddings were yelling, the wagon was tilting and swaying, turning slowly as it was pushed by an icy wind and claimed by an insistent current —

The first of the Diggers burst onto the riverbank and O'Brien drew his Colt and shot him in the chest. A sudden ripple of small-arms fire spat at them from the receding shore and he screamed at them all to get down as low as they could. An arrow slapped into the canvas awning overhead.

But they were moving faster now, leaving the Indians behind, drifting further out into the centre of the river and turning sluggishly towards the west, and they weren't sinking, not a bit of it, they were gliding, rocking ever so slightly to the push of a bracing wind . . . and leaving the Indians, the oxen, O'Brien's trusty mount, behind them.

Boosted by the wintry gale, the wagon dipped and yawed just like the schooners after which it was named. But because the box was watertight, because it had been built to cross rivers and streams as well as prairies, it bobbed on like a cork, and through the gathered canvas at the rear they saw the Diggers shrink rapidly to doll-size, and heard the angry crack of their old weapons diminish to nothing more dangerous than a string of ineffectual pops.

They swung drunkenly around a bend and the Indians vanished from sight.

At last the bundled children began to

calm down and sense that they weren't going to die after all, that they were actually embarking on the first leg of their escape from these cloistering mountains, and without warning, Conway suddenly grabbed O'Brien and hugged him with a wild euphoria.

'We've done it, O'Brien! Lord Almighty, we've done it! Well done, man, this is down to you!'

O'Brien, quivering a bit now that it was quite literally behind them, had no sooner leathered his Colt than Eddings was pumping his hand. But ever cautious, O'Brien said, 'Take it easy, you men . . . take it easy, all of you. We're not out of the woods yet.'

Rose's pale, pinched face tightened quickly. 'Yes, yes . . . you're right. This place Oroville . . . it's still quite a way away, isn't it?'

He looked down the wagon at them all. The wagon-box was dim, claustrophobic, a little stuffy. 'Sixty, seventy miles,' he replied.

'Do you think the wagon can

withstand the journey?' asked Kate.

'If we're careful,' he said. 'If we make sure we don't run aground and hole it.'

He eased forward, straddled the seat, put one big fist around the erect wagon-tongue and watched the current ahead of them, a restless brown course enclosed by two bands of dark green timber.

'Seventy miles,' muttered Eddings, almost savoring the relatively short distance. 'How soon do you suppose we can make it?'

Two days,' O'Brien responded. 'Maybe a little more. That's taking it in stages, keeping roughly to the centre of the river to avoid any obstacles, finding safe places to tie up after dark and so that you and your young 'uns can stretch your legs.'

Conway said emotionally, 'Mr. O'Brien . . . you know we can never even *begin* to repay you for this.'

'Forget it, Conway. You never know, there might come a day when I need *your* help. But keep that sapling handy

— you too, Eddings. Could be we'll need 'em in a hurry if we start drifting too close to shore.'

The Conestoga averaged a speed of eight or nine miles every hour, but by mid-afternoon several of the children turned bilious and, with early darkness already powdering the sky, O'Brien snagged an overhanging bough with his lariat and brought them to an unsteady halt.

By trial and error, they finally managed to secure the wagon back and front, and haul it in to a snowy clearing. Later, with everyone on shore and warming themselves by a blazing fire, they cooked up coffee and, when the prospect of food no longer turned the stomach quite so sour, they ate.

They pushed on through the bleak mountains the following day, the going slower now as the current turned more torpid, and rocked and bounced through a violent snowstorm that lasted for most of the morning. Seasickness was still a problem, mostly for the children, but when the afternoon cleared and cool sunshine slanted down through the scudding clouds to lighten the otherwise cheerless wagon-box, their spirits lifted a little.

Once again, O'Brien found that the long darkness hours restricted their travelling time, but because their progress was good they made no complaint. They spent their second night on snowy banks and shoved off again the following morning. By this time the wagon was beginning to list a bit, and make ominous creaking sounds as it rode the white-water current south and west.

Around the middle of that day the river narrowed down and Conway spotted strings of wood smoke hanging above a broad sweep of timber around the next lazy bend. Although they all knew what it must signify, they were almost afraid to come right out and say it.

An hour later, however, they drifted

into Oroville, and for the greenhorns it was all finally *over*.

Like most folks in times of crisis or unusual circumstance, the people of Oroville proved to be good, charitable souls who quickly rallied around once the story of the greenhorns' flight from the mountains got out. The Conways and the Eddings were taken in, given access to tin tubs and steaming water, and handed-down clothes were donated to replace the rags their original garments had become. That night they slept with a roof over their heads, and the following day O'Brien arranged to borrow a wagon — their own was little more than junk wood projecting from the river by this time — so that they could begin the chain-rattling twenty-mile drive south to Scot's Post.

Their arrival in Scot's Post later that same afternoon caused an immediate buzz, but O'Brien stopped for no one until Peter McGovern's store hove into sight. Then he hauled back on the steaming team-horses and helped

Conway and Eddings get the women and children down, and there on the porch outside McGovern's store there followed a reunion that was guaranteed to moisten the eyes of practically everyone who was there to witness it.

Tearfully McGovern herded them all inside, O'Brien included. The store was cluttered with provision-packed shelves and warmed by a centrally-situated pot-bellied stove. O'Brien stood apart from the family as they all hugged each other and the greenhorns assured the storekeeper that they were all right, and Mrs. McGovern dispensed candy sticks to the slightly baffled children.

Finally there was a moment of silence as they remembered Alice Eddings and the scout, Joe Coldeway.

Into the silence came Milt Frazier, the town marshal, who had gotten word of their arrival but plainly had never really expected to see it. He too was immediately drawn into the reunion, but quickly broke away in order to hurry over to O'Brien and shake him warmly by the hand.

'By God, O'Brien, I never thought you'd do it, but I guess all them stories they tell about you must be true after all, eh?' The youngish man, muffled against the brisk, blue-sky day, looked around and the brows above his pleasant eyes suddenly lowered in a frown. 'Say, where's Charlie Button?'

O'Brien looked at him and shook his head. 'Charlie didn't make it,' he said quietly.

A look of real pain altered Frazier's thin face and he muttered, 'Aw, hell. Charlie was a good man.'

'One of the best. If it hadn't been for him — '

McGovern suddenly appeared from the back of the store with a fancy green bottle in his hands, and called for quiet. 'Come along now, mother,' he said to his wife. 'Pass those glasses around. This here is real, gen-u-ine San Mateo champagne. I've been saving it for . . . ' he swallowed thickly, ' . . . for an occasion like this.'

He worked the top for a moment, as an expectant silence fell over the gathering, and then the cork popped out and flew across the room and the children gasped in awe as effervescent white froth spilled out over the bottle-neck.

At exactly that same moment a voice outside the store yelled, 'O'Brien!'

The store fell silent again but for the sound of champagne dribbling wetly off the bottle to puddle on the floor. The adults looked at each other, sensing from the tone of the voice that whoever was out there was hardly part of a welcoming committee.

O'Brien looked steadily at Frazier, whose thin face seemed to age before him. 'That's one of the things I came here to tell you,' the marshal said in a low tone. 'John Bragg and his cronies been hangin' around town the past week or so. I don't reckon they thought you'd ever make it back, but it's plain enough they figured to be here in case you *did*.'

O'Brien echoed the name bitterly. *Bragg.*

He nodded slowly, aware that McGovern and the greenhorns were watching him, the greenhorns clearly mystified because they knew nothing of the trouble he'd had here a week and a half earlier. 'I've had my fill of killing,' he said softly, 'but I don't suppose it'd do much good if you were to go out there and post them out of town again, would it?'

Frazier's now-troubled eyes slid away from his weather-burned face. 'It's like I said before,' he replied uncomfortably. 'The Braggs do pretty much whatever they want around here.'

'Yeah,' O'Brien said sourly. 'Like you said.' He looked at the closed door, then reached down, unbuttoned his sheepskin jacket, hitched his gunbelt around, lifted the .38 out and then let it drop back into the holster. He sighed tiredly. 'All right, Frazier. Stand aside.'

Conway came forward. 'What's this all about, Mr. O'Brien?'

O'Brien glanced at him. 'Nothing that need concern you,' he replied. 'But I'd be obliged if you and your people'd keep away from the windows for the next couple of minutes.'

'Keep . . . ?'

O'Brien went past him, boot falls hollow on the plank floor. On impulse Frazier called his name and he stopped, looked back over one shoulder. Awkwardly, Frazier shook his head and croaked shamefully, 'Nothin'.'

O'Brien smiled coolly. 'I thought not.'

He opened the door and let himself out onto the boardwalk.

The Braggs were fanned out in the middle of the street directly in front of the store; big, awkward-moving John, with his close-set, mean brown eyes and the sneer-snarl mouth beneath his bushy, untidy moustache; the Quinn brothers, his cousins; Tom, funereal in black, the color accentuating the paleness of his face, the white blondness of his wispy beard, and big, blond,

hollow-eyed, slashed-mouthed Aaron;
and finally Rafael da Silva, the whip-
slim, good-looking political assassin and
gunman.

O'Brien saw that Bragg held a coil of
rope in his meaty fists.

He planted himself on the boardwalk
in front of them, legs slightly parted for
balance, jacket brushed back for easier
access to his Colt, eyes beneath the
shade of his hat revealing nothing save
possibly distaste for the quartet arrayed
before him.

Around them the town was still,
Main Street unusually deserted. The
wind moaned softly, toyed with hat-
brims, brushed the loosest, most
powdery snow off the tops of the
chunky drifts that lined the thoroughfare.

At last John Bragg said, 'We got some
unfinished business, O'Brien.'

O'Brien shook his head. 'I've got no
business with you. With any of you.'

'You killed my brother,' Bragg
reminded him.

'And you fellers tried to ambush me and Charlie Button up in the foothills last week,' O'Brien countered. 'Reckon that's why you've got your left arm bandaged up, Aaron. Charlie and me were sure we'd hit at least one of you.' He returned his eyeline to Bragg. 'I figure that makes us even.'

Bragg shook his head. 'Not in my book.'

O'Brien looked him right in the eye, saw a readiness, a willingness, a desire there, to kill. 'Maybe we ought to rewrite the book, then,' he said gravely.

'No need,' said Bragg. 'We said we was gunna hang you, and that's what we're gunna do.'

O'Brien let his right hand hover over the butt of the .38. 'Well, if you boys think I'm coming without an argument, you'd better think again.'

Aaron Quinn said contemptuously, 'Figure you can take all four of us, O'Brien?'

O'Brien raised one shoulder. 'I don't see why not. I reckon the four of you together still don't add up to one of me.'

Bragg stiffened and his face seemed suddenly to evict every emotion save hatred. 'All right,' he said, flinging down the rope and adopting a gunfighter's stance. 'If that's the way you want it.'

'It's not,' O'Brien answered. 'But a man plays the cards the way they fall, I guess.'

The door swung open behind O'Brien just then, and Marshal Frazier came hesitantly out onto the porch to stand beside him.

'You . . . ' He had trouble speaking, and had to clear his throat before he could start afresh.

'You know I can't let you do this, Big John,' he said.

Bragg scowled at him. 'I don't know what you're gunna do to stop it,' he replied impatiently. 'Now just you turn around and go back inside and you won't get hurt in the overspill.'

Frazier shook his head. 'Can't do

that, John,' he replied.

'Don't matter to us anyway, Milt,' said da Silva in heavily accented English. 'You're still outnumbered two to one.'

'I . . . ' Another swallow. 'I'll take my chances alongside O'Brien.'

'Me, too.'

The door creaked open again, and Arthur Conway came out onto the porch with his repeater athwart his chest. O'Brien glanced at him as he came to a halt on the other side of him and he hissed through closed teeth, 'Get back inside, Conway. This isn't your fight.'

Conway looked absolutely terrified, but when he spoke there was real grit in his voice. 'After what you did for my family and me, your fight's my fight, I reckon.'

Eddings came out to join them then, and went to stand beside his brother-in-law with rifle in hand. McGovern came next, and lined up beside the marshal with a big .45 in his fist, and then Kate

Eddings appeared, hefting an oily pistol she appeared to have taken direct from McGovern's stock. When she squeezed in between O'Brien and Conway, the line-up was complete.

Inside, O'Brien fought a war with his emotions. On the one hand he was angry that these people should ally themselves with him. If it should come to a shooting fight, as seemed likely, he could do without having to worry about their safety. And yet on the other hand he appreciated their loyalty, the knowledge that they thought as much of him as they evidently did.

In any case, there was no going back on it now; what was done, was done. Without taking his eyes off Bragg he said, 'Well, how do you like the way the odds're shaping up now, Big John? All of a sudden, it's six guns against four.' He looked up and down the street, at the townsfolk who were beginning to appear at windows and doorways. 'You stick around much longer and I might just get me a whole army.'

A man who ran the emporium next door suddenly appeared on his boardwalk, an old Spencer carbine in his hands, his wife still struggling to haul him back out of the line of fire.

'You can't fight the whole town, Bragg,' O'Brien went on, stating fact. 'You know, it could just be that you've bullied these people once too often.'

'You're callin' it right, feller,' called the emporium-owner. 'We just about had a gutful of it, I say.'

Bragg glared at him, turned slowly to rake his cold, unforgiving eyes across the storefronts lining both sides of Main. The wind blew some more snow-dust off the drifts. Wood smoke touched his nostrils. At length he returned his glare to O'Brien. 'You might think you've won,' he sneered, 'but you haven't. It don't end as simple as all that, O'Brien.'

O'Brien shook his head. 'That's where you're wrong, Bragg. It *has* ended. For you.' Suddenly his eyes went absolutely flat. 'Now get out of town, all of you. Right, marshal?'

Frazier inclined his head. 'Right, O'Brien. Things're changing here, Big John. If you've got any sense, you'll change with 'em.'

Bragg held his gaze a moment longer, then bent, snatched up his rope and spun away to stalk down towards the livery stable with his cousins hurrying after him. The Mexican gunman lingered for one more moment, then turned slowly and swaggered away. Within minutes the Braggs came out of the stable astride their horses, and rode out of town at a sour-tempered, snow-churning gallop.

The sense of relief that washed through the people who had come to O'Brien's aid was a palpable, weakening thing. McGovern sagged against a porch post, called a thank-you to his neighbor for his support. Gratefully he and the greenhorns went back into the store, leaving O'Brien and Frazier on the boardwalk, Frazier jumpy and animated now that the confrontation was over.

'You know somethin'?' he said. 'I think we might just have turned a corner here. I got me a feelin' that them Braggs'll think twice before they start throwing their weight around Scot's Post again.'

O'Brien shrugged. 'Could be you're right,' he said skeptically. 'Anyway, one thing's certain-sure. I'm grateful to you, Frazier. All of you. I know it couldn't have been easy.'

'There's not much in this life that is,' Frazier replied, but he was obviously pleased with the praise.

As they went back into the store, O'Brien threw a last look at the brooding Sierra Nevada, fanging the cloudless blue sky with its jagged peaks.

Inside, McGovern and his wife had distributed glasses of rapidly flattening champagne to their relations and those children who were old enough to chance a sip. As O'Brien came in and closed the door behind him, Kate

Eddings handed him a glass and behind his counter, Peter McGovern cleared his throat.

'Don't worry,' he said. 'This won't take long. I just want for us to take a moment to remember the people who can't be with us here today. Jimmy's dear wife Alice. Your David, who's still recuperating up at Doc Winner's place. Our own dear friend Charlie Button.

'Your scout, Coldeway. Let's drink a toast to their memory and David's courage, and to the hope that you good people will be able to put everything you've been through behind you and find yourselves a good life here in Scot's Post.

'But most of all I . . . I'd like for us to toast the health of a fine, determined, upstanding man without whom you would have undoubtedly perished in the mountains, a man without whom I wouldn't have had my family restored to me . . . '

He looked down into his glass and blinked several times, until he had his feelings back under control. Then, with renewed strength, McGovern lifted his head and looked O'Brien straight in the face, and as he raised his glass he said formally, 'Ladies and gentlemen . . . boys and girls . . . I give you . . . O'Brien.'

The greenhorns turned slowly to look at him, raised their glasses in his direction, then echoed the toast with feeling.

'O'Brien!'

'O'Brien!'

'*O'Brien!*'

We do hope that you have enjoyed
reading this large print book.

Did you know that all of our titles
are available for purchase?

We publish a wide range of high
quality large print books including:
Romances, Mysteries, Classics
General Fiction
Non Fiction and Westerns

Special interest titles available in
large print are:
The Little Oxford Dictionary
Music Book, Song Book
Hymn Book, Service Book

Also available from us courtesy of
Oxford University Press:
Young Readers' Dictionary
(large print edition)
Young Readers' Thesaurus
(large print edition)

For further information or a free
brochure, please contact us at:
Ulverscroft Large Print Books Ltd.,
The Green, Bradgate Road, Anstey,
Leicester, LE7 7FU, England.
Tel: (00 44) **0116 236 4325**
Fax: (00 44) **0116 234 0205**

COFFIN FOR AN OUTLAW

Thomas McNulty

When legendary lawman-turned-bounty-hunter Chance Sonnet reappears, the word spreads that he wants Eric Cabot dead. Cabot, in the dark as to Sonnet's motives, sends his men to kill Sonnet first — but the task proves more difficult than he imagines. Sonnet also finds himself pursued by a plucky newspaperwoman and an old Texas Ranger who knows something of his past. Blazing a trail in a buckboard and hauling a pine coffin intended for Cabot, Chance Sonnet is a man haunted by the past and facing a future steeped in blood.

A TOWN CALLED INNOCENCE

Simon Webb

Falsely convicted of murder and sentenced to hang, it seems as though the end of young Will Bennett's life is in sight — but a strange circumstance of fate frees him to track down the real murderer. His journey takes him to a Texas town where he learns the truth about the plot that nearly sent him to the gallows. Bennett's journey from the town called Innocence to the final showdown with the man who framed him for murder ends in a bloody shootout, from which only one man will emerge alive.

INVITATION TO A FUNERAL

Jethro Kyle

At twenty-eight, Joseph Carver is the youngest college professor in the United States. He is estranged from his father Will, the sheriff of a Kansas town. When Will is gunned down during a bank robbery and Joseph's mother dies of grief shortly thereafter, he is forced to face his family demons and return home. After his parents' funeral, he arms himself and sets off in pursuit of the men who shot his father. His quest takes him into the Indian Nations, where he receives help of a most surprising nature . . .

MEXICAN MERCY MISSION

Richard Smith

After Sam's parents and sister are murdered by four bandits in a raid on their Texas homestead, the seventeen-year-old decides to ride south with his uncle, Marshal William Grant. Sam is determined to avenge the deaths of his family members. Across the Mexican border, they talk their way into a fortified hideout with the ambitious hope of rescuing a young girl who has been abducted by the same four killers. And on the way home, pursued relentlessly across the Rio Grande by bandits, they must face one final bloody battle . . .

COYOTE MOON

Ralph Hayes

Buffalo hunter O'Brien is settling down to a more civilized life in Fort Revenge, in Indian Territory, helping his friend run a stage line there. However, it isn't long before trouble comes from two directions: in the form of an outlaw gang from Tulsa who want to buy his friend's stagecoach company and won't take no for an answer, and from a family of killers who are seeking revenge for the death of their kin at his hands. O'Brien must respond to these challenges with his own brand of gunsmoke . . .